CHARLO...
CHARLOT...

Y0-EFV-677

WINTER LIGHTS

•

JAN McDANIEL

AVALON BOOKS
THOMAS BOUREGY AND COMPANY, INC.
401 LAFAYETTE STREET
NEW YORK, NEW YORK 10003

© Copyright 1996 by Jan McDaniel
Library of Congress Catalog Card Number: 95-96215
ISBN 0-8034-9162-X
All rights reserved.
All the characters in this book are fictitious,
and any resemblance to actual persons,
living or dead, is purely coincidental.

PRINTED IN THE UNITED STATES OF AMERICA
ON ACID-FREE PAPER
BY HADDON CRAFTSMEN, SCRANTON, PENNSYLVANIA

Chapter One

The brightly lit Victorian house glowed like a beacon in the frozen night. Two giant plastic candy canes flanked the entrance, smoke curled from the chimney, and the sound of happy voices and holiday music drifted outside. Christmas lights strung around the roof cast multicolor reflections in the Wisconsin snow.

Anyone else would have found the party inside a pleasant refuge from the wintry darkness. But despite the welcoming atmosphere, Kate Smithers hesitated, halting on the walkway out front. She stared at the home of her parents' oldest and dearest friends, the Dunmores, as the stinging wind whipped mercilessly at her legs through her thin hose.

A party. She'd always loved people and gatherings,

especially during the holidays. Now, the prospect of stepping inside only intensified the dull ache in her heart. Mingling with people required tremendous effort these days. But she was determined to do it, determined to make herself feel normal again.

Her father came up beside her, placing a hand on her shoulder and studying her inquisitively.

Kate forced an apologetic smile. ''I'm not ready for this,'' she explained.

Her mother, looking worried, stepped forward. ''You've always enjoyed the Dunmores' parties, Kate,'' Julia Smithers reminded her daughter. ''These are people you've known all your life.''

But I'm different now, Katie thought.

She stared at the gaily lit house as though it were a dungeon she was being forced into. Suddenly, she longed for the sanctuary of her parents' house on a quiet Saturday night alone with a good book or a video.

But even though her stomach was churning, she knew sooner or later she was going to have to face people, meet their stares. The plane crash hadn't left any visible scars, but she didn't know whether the wounds inside would ever heal.

She forced a deep breath.

The sound of laughter from inside chimed on the night air, and Kate put a hand to her stomach. She just didn't know if she could bear all that happiness.

''We don't have to stay long,'' her mother coaxed.

"But you've come this far, and the Dunmores are anxious to see you again."

"Everybody is," her father added.

Kate's look darkened. She knew this was a mistake. She was starting out too fast, jumping in among too many people at once. She wasn't ready. Agreeing to come tonight had been a hasty decision—one she regretted now.

"The party's success doesn't hinge on my appearance," she concluded, grateful she'd brought her own car and no one would have to drive her home. "Please make my apologies to Ina and Claude. I don't feel well. Really."

Ashamed at having disappointed her parents but unable to help it, she'd taken two steps backward when the front door burst open and a streak of blue shot out. It stopped as abruptly as it had appeared, perching at the top of the porch steps. Kate realized the form was a young man with shaggy blond hair. He was dressed in jeans and a denim shirt.

He was staring at her, his eyes widening with recognition and his mouth slanting in a lopsided grin. "Kate! I thought that was you I saw out here. You're late, but I suppose we can overlook that this once."

She squinted as she peered at him. He looked vaguely familiar, but . . .

"Noel?" she asked incredulously. Last time she'd seen him, he'd still been a gangly teenager, not the tall handsome man standing before her.

He stepped down off the porch, taking long strides toward her, and Kate thought he must be freezing since he wasn't wearing a coat.

He swooped over her and wrapped her in a bear hug, holding her several seconds before releasing her. "It's good to see you. You wouldn't believe the stories floating around about your becoming a hermit."

Over her shoulder, Kate saw her dad delivering Noel a warning look, shaking his head.

Her brow furrowed. "A hermit?" she asked, laughing lightly at the image of herself in shredded overalls and a straw hat, building campfires in the woods. She turned to Norman Smithers. "It's all right, Dad," she assured him. It was difficult to remain defensive amid Noel's easy friendliness. Even when she used to baby-sit him, he'd been a happy-go-lucky kid. Maybe his casual cheerfulness was what she needed. She already felt a little better.

"You should know better than to listen to that small-town gossip," she chided him. "And then to come outside without a coat on."

"It's your fault," he countered. "If you were inside, I wouldn't have to be out here. Come on. Mom and Dad will be tickled to see you. It's not every day we're visited by the rich and famous."

Feeling as though she'd swallowed a chunk of lead, Kate closed her eyes. Noel was, of course, exaggerating her success. Until a few weeks ago, she'd believed she was realizing her dreams. Now, everything that had seemed so important only made her feel cold inside. She feared she had lost her drive. All she wanted now was a place where she felt safe.

He tossed a long arm over her shoulders and led her up the walkway. Her parents trailed behind them.

Kate didn't see any means of escape.

She glanced sideways at Noel. "I thought you were away at school."

"Even lowly med students get a Christmas break."

"You need a haircut, you know," she teased.

He shook the locks that curled just above his collar. "Give me a break, Kate, please. I'm on vacation."

Reaching the door, Kate felt a rush of panic. She didn't want to dampen everyone's evening. When they saw her, they would think immediately of death, of the plane crash and the victim who didn't survive.

She looked up at Noel. When had he gotten so tall? He smiled encouragingly. She realized he was probably the one person in town who expected her to be the same as she'd always been, years ago when she'd lived here. She didn't want to shatter his expectations.

But if she got over this, next time it would have to be easier, she reasoned. Noel swung open the front door, stepped aside, and bowed. "Milady." He waited for her to enter.

Kate rolled her eyes, but cast him a grateful smile. Taking a deep breath, she crossed the threshold.

*   *   *

"I hate to see old Hewett Sparks coast into the mayor's office unopposed for another term," Chandler McCorey, owner of the local feed store, told Grady Meredith and Libby Drew.

Grady, towering nearly a full foot over Libby, shot Chandler a wry smile. The merchant had to be pushing seventy himself. "Hewett might move a little slow, but he's been mayor as long as I can remember," he observed.

Chandler hooted. "My point exactly. And what has he done for this town? Pure nothin'. I'd say he's had plenty of time to make some changes. No, Grady, what Shady Pointe needs is progressive thinking, some young blood. Someone who's not afraid to get up out of a chair and shake things up. Someone like you, Grady. Folks respect you around here, and you know this town inside and out."

Chandler pulled at the stiff collar of his white shirt. Tonight was one of the rare occasions he'd traded his standard flannel shirt and coveralls for more formal attire. His discomfort was obvious.

Libby, looking up, beamed at Grady beside her. "What a wonderful idea," she agreed, half teasing, half serious. "You'd make a fine mayor, Grady."

Grady cleared his throat, then cast Libby a dubious look. He turned back to the older man. "Much as I appreciate your confidence in me, Chandler," he ventured, "I'm no politician. I've got my hands full with my veterinary practice."

Chandler dropped his voice. "Trouble is, Hewett and his friends have been running things so long, as long as he's comfortable, nothing is going to change. Nobody in this town who's not in with that bunch can get anything done. You know Mabel Osgood?"

Rubbing his chin, Grady nodded. "Everyone in town knows Mabel."

"That woman works magic with a needle and thread. Makes some of the prettiest things I've ever seen. Lost her husband ten years ago and doesn't have much money to live off of, although every time you turn around, you see her helping somebody out. Anyway, a few months ago she got the idea from some magazine to open a little shop in the front of her house, sell baby clothes and fancy dresses for little girls. She's got that big old place right off the downtown area on Maple Street, plenty of extra rooms, and folks buy stuff from her off and on anyway."

"Sounds like an enterprising idea," Grady mused. "What happened?"

"The police chief came around and closed her down, told her her property wasn't zoned for business."

"All she's got to do . . ." Grady began.

Chandler cut him off. "The zoning board won't approve it. You see Martha Trent, who owns the boutique downtown, is Evie Sparks' old pal. Are you making the connection?"

"That boutique has only a small corner with children's clothing that I've noticed, and everything in there is overpriced,'' Libby noted. ''I'd love to see some new stores open here.''

Chandler shook his head. ''Don't look for that to happen. Most of the local folks are so frustrated, they've given up trying. Old Sparks is killing this town. Strangling it slowly. He and his friends control everything. It ain't right, Grady.''

''He should be about ready to retire,'' Grady noted optimistically.

''When he does, his son Dan will run.'' Chandler stepped closer to Grady, lowering his voice almost to a whisper. ''We can't wait and see what happens. My nephew Toby sells real estate over in Milwaukee, and he's got a client interested in building a development along Echo Lake. Summer cabins, hunting lodges, and retirement homes for people who could bring some money and maybe some energy into this town. But if the city jerks this fella around about water and access to the dump and fire protection, there are a hundred other little hungry towns with pretty lakes in this area. For myself, I don't care either way, but I've got kids and grandkids living here. I'd like to see them all stay and be able to make a go of it.''

''Maybe Sparks does need some opposition, but why me?'' Grady asked. ''I own property out at Echo Lake, and I'm not sure I want hordes of yuppies and retirees swarming over the place. Besides, I don't want to be in the spotlight.''

"First off, you've got the grit to stand up to him. And you've got charisma. People will vote for you."

Grady chuckled, the corners of his eyes crinkling. "Charisma? With four-legged critters maybe."

Looking up at him, Libby twisted the glass of ginger ale she held in one hand. The lights on the nearby Christmas tree reflected in the amber liquid.

"You do have that suave all-American charm," she cajoled. "And Chandler is right. The schools are having a hard time recruiting teachers, and even more difficulty getting any to stay once they're here. Nobody wants to settle in a place where there's little to do and no opportunity."

"Small towns are supposed to be boring," Grady maintained. "That's their charm. I like it here exactly because it *is* quiet."

Libby tossed her head back. "People want peace and quiet, not drudgery. If they give up the theater and museums, they need something to compensate for that."

"They can walk in the woods, spend the morning fishing, go swimming or ice-skating."

"Not everyone grew up tuned in to those kinds of solitary activities," Libby reminded him.

Grady glanced down at his companion, raising one dark eyebrow. "You're not thinking of leaving, are you?" he asked.

Having intended his comment as a joke, he was startled by Libby's solemn expression.

"I'm looking at some teaching offers for next year," she said, studying the glass.

Before Grady could advise her to not make any hasty decisions, he grew aware of a sudden hush falling over the room. He looked up to see the other guests staring into the Dunmores' foyer, and followed their glances.

The unexpected sight of Kate Smithers rocked him. She'd just come in, Noel Dunmore hanging on to her like a kid coaxing a stray puppy to follow him home. Kate's parents stepped in behind them.

Katie, he thought, a nostalgic wave of tenderness rolling through his chest involuntarily. He hadn't seen her in seven or eight years, though he knew she'd recently come home.

"Now look there," Chandler said, waving his glass in her direction. "Shady Pointe's most successful hometown girl. She had to go all the way to New York to make her fortune. Shame about that accident though."

Grady scarcely heard him. He knew all too well Katie had gone elsewhere to build her future. Despite the rumors he'd heard around town, she didn't look beaten. Since he'd last seen her, she'd blossomed from a classically pretty girl with high, aristocratic cheekbones into an enchanting woman. It was no wonder she'd recently been a very successful model. Her creamy complexion was flushed from the cold, and her long lashes fluttered softly over the lightest blue eyes

To Kate, the sudden silence ripped through the room like a passing locomotive. She was aware of the stillness; on the stereo, "Let It Snow" sounded louder now that the voices had faded. Everyone was looking at her, waiting for her to break into a thousand tiny little pieces.

So many people here. She was suffocating, her legs threatening not to hold her. Her impulse was to bolt out the door, but she resolved to be strong. Her life had to go on, no matter how she felt inside.

Without realizing it, she'd been leaning against Noel.

Gently, she twisted away from him. His mom hurried over to them. "Good evening Kate, Julia, Norman. I'm so glad you could make it." She turned fond eyes back to Kate. "And especially you, missy. You've been avoiding us far too long."

Kate squelched the lump that rose in her throat as Ina gave her a warm hug. She hated feeling so raw, so childish. Would she ever be the same again?

She rubbed her hands together. "I've missed all of you," she told their hostess.

"Kate's been so busy," Julia Smithers defended her daughter.

Noel rolled his eyes. "Yeah, we read it about it in the *Wall Street Journal*."

Kate waved him off. "No biggie," she said quickly.

"Would you like something to eat or drink?" Ina offered, gesturing toward a lavish buffet table. A fully decorated miniature Christmas tree served as the centerpiece.

"Not just now, thanks," Kate declined. She couldn't eat with her stomach in knots.

"I'll see that she eats before she leaves," Noel promised, snaring Kate's hand in his. He turned to Kate, flashing her a conspiratorial wink. "Come on out to the back porch and meet my friends," he offered. "We've kind of migrated out there, away from the old folks."

Kate caught her mother's uneasy expression. "I'll be fine, Mom," she assured her. She knew Julia was remembering her hesitation outside.

Escaping with Noel was actually a relief. He treated her as though nothing were wrong, and it made her feel better. Her parents had been good and patient ever since she'd come back, but she was twenty-eight years old, far too mature to revert back to her childhood. She wasn't so sure how Noel's friends were going to react to her though.

A hum had picked up among the guests; glasses clinked and voices buzzed once again. Kate held her shoulders stiff as she passed through the crowd, knowing despite the resumption of party noises that curious eyes were aimed her way.

She didn't hear the speculation, but she felt it, like cold water running through her. News of the crash had been carried on television and in the papers. They were all wondering what it was like to survive such an ordeal, wondering, as she was, why she had escaped unscathed while another died. Unfortunately, because she owned a large, successful company, the press had blown what reporters termed a miracle and she considered a fluke way beyond its rightful proportions.

Though her heart was missing beats, she met the stares, forcing her smile in place.

When her eyes fell on a familiar face not focused on her, her heart lurched. Grady Meredith stood along the far wall beside the tinsel-laden Christmas tree, intently engaged in a conversation with Mr. McCorey, the feed store owner, and a petite woman with short blond hair who was a stranger to Kate. Whatever they were discussing had Mr. McCorey worked up. His face was as red as holly berries.

Grady was even easier to look at than she remembered. His finely etched features were topped by slightly wavy dark-brown hair, his thick eyebrows bobbing animatedly as their discussion progressed. Tall and self-assured, he leaned slightly to one side, his arm draped amicably around the short woman's shoulders.

Although Kate had exorcised her memories of Grady years ago, an unwarranted pang of jealousy stabbed her. She could have been the one nestled in the crook of his arm right now. It appeared to be such a comfortable shelter.

Without warning, his glance swung in her direction,

his alert brown eyes settling on her. Warmth mingled with her shock, and she saw a faint softening in his expression. He didn't indicate any surprise at seeing her. She wondered whether his memories of her were kind or bitter. It was just like Grady to find the best in anyone, even her after she'd broken her promise. . . . But he'd left her no choice.

Realizing she'd lost her forced smile, she managed a real one for him.

In return, he sent her a heart-wrenching grin. His eyes trailed briefly to his companions, as if silently explaining why he couldn't step forward to speak to her.

Her stomach clenched at the prospect of an encounter with him. She definitely wasn't ready for that. The last thing she could tolerate tonight, or ever, was his pity.

Diverting her gaze, she quickened her step. A reunion with Grady and an introduction to his friend weren't on her agenda this evening.

Pausing, Noel turned to her. ''Still with me?'' he asked.

Realizing she had his hand in a death grip, she loosened her grasp.

''Sorry,'' she apologized.

His friends were clustered around the antique wood-burning stove on the spacious, glass-enclosed back porch. Moonlight reflected on the snow-draped yard,

that bordered on silver. Her reddish-brown hair was painstakingly upswept, revealing the sapphire studs dotting each earlobe.

But Grady knew Katie was more than just a beauty. Her business sense had enabled her to start her own company, one that let her indulge her flair for design and love of dolls. The Calico Chrissie doll was a top seller across the country.

Katie was smiling as she deposited her coat into the waiting arms of their hostess, Ina Dunmore, who had rushed to the door to greet her special guest with a hug. The midnight blue wool dress Kate wore was lined with shimmering sequins at the bodice and accented her slender figure.

Grady caught his breath. She was striking, stunning, poised, and obviously successful. He still thought of her as the fireball in cutoffs, a baggy T-shirt, and tennis shoes, whose ponytail streamed out from beneath her baseball cap as she danced around the bases after belting a softball to the fence. She'd had a powerful swing.

The other, more painful memories, he'd driven from his mind long ago: slow dancing in the park pavilion on a summer night, watching her eyes light up as she devoured a cherry-vanilla ice-cream cone, kissing her as sunset splashed patches of red across Echo Lake. That part of the past he refused to dwell on now or any other time.

He'd never considered her fragile. But as he studied

her, he sensed an underlying nervousness beneath the broad smile and the proudly tilting chin. Even from this distance, he sensed a vulnerability in her eyes he'd never seen before. He'd seen that look a thousand times in the eyes of frightened animals, but he'd never expected it in Katie.

It was obvious that the plane crash, while not damaging her physically, had taken a toll on her psyche. And all the attendant, relentless coverage from the media must not have helped. Katie was a hot story— beautiful former model and successful businesswoman survives tragic plane crash.

They'd parted ways long ago. He told himself the fresh concern rising in him stemmed not from unresolved emotions but his instinct to soothe wounded spirits.

Glancing down, he caught Libby watching him with concern. As he realized he'd been staring, he gave Libby a reassuring smile and returned his attention to their conversation.

"I don't think anything could have kept Katie from leaving, Chandler," he noted. "But, hey, how about *you* running for mayor?"

Chandler guffawed. "An old grouch like me? And wear a tie every day?" He pawed at his collar, then narrowed his eyes and lowered his voice. "I will if I have to, but there's not much point to running a candidate who'll never win."

*   *   *

providing a spectacular view. Outside, tiny snowflakes swirled beneath the floodlights.

"This porch didn't used to be here," she told Noel.

"My parents had it built on a few years ago. Best part of the house, I think."

"It's cozy," she agreed. "But I am sorry to see it's snowing again."

"I love the snow," he countered, blond hair falling across his forehead. "Come on, let me introduce you to everybody."

She noticed that several of Noel's friends eyed her warily, but overall, they seemed to take their cues from him and received her casually. A few of them she remembered from earlier days here in Shady Pointe. The others were from nearby towns.

Although Noel acted as though the four-year gap in their ages no longer existed, Kate noted his friends addressed her with the polite reserve they might give a teacher or an aunt.

Back here, away from the rest of the party, she began to relax. No one seemed to be expecting anything from her. When the introductions were over, the previous conversations resumed.

Noel, standing in front of her, leaned forward. "Can I get you something to drink now, Kate? Mom doesn't like any of her guests wandering around without a glass in one hand."

"You don't have to spend all your time with me,

Noel.'' She'd noticed more than one young woman watching him with interest.

''Don't be silly. You're not tired of me already, are you?''

''Of course not.''

''What can I get you? Eggnog?''

''Just a cola or something would be fine. Thanks.''

''I'll be right back.''

As she stood watching him walk off, the pressure of a hand on her shoulder made her jump.

She swung around and found herself looking into Grady Meredith's warm, penetrating brown eyes. The heat of his hand radiated through the fabric of her dress.

He was the last person she was prepared to face tonight. But she supposed she should have known that when she came back to Shady Pointe, this meeting was inevitable. All she could do now was get this over with as quickly as possible.

Gazing up at him, struggling not to get caught up in those eyes she'd once found irresistible, she swallowed her nervousness and stiffened her spine.

Chapter Two

"Whoa." He attempted to calm her, coming up close behind her, tightening his grip on her shoulder, and leaning forward. She caught a whiff of spicy after-shave. "It's only me."

Her heart was drumming just as it had back in high school whenever he was nearby. Good grief, after all this time and everything that had happened, how could she have such an adolescent reaction?

She felt ridiculous to have been so skittish. Well, here was her chance to make it clear she hadn't returned in hopes of disrupting his life.

She turned to him. Mercifully, his hand dropped from her shoulder.

His eyes skimmed over her approvingly, and she

wished he'd quit looking at her like that. Her stomach was doing flip-flops, her heart quivering.

She took a step back.

"How have you been, Kate?" he asked.

She raised her chin. "You know me—I always bounce back." She didn't have it in her to lie and say she was fine, but she wasn't about to admit her problems to him. "It's been a long time, Grady. How are you?"

"Good." His eyes swept over her again. "It's been too long, Kate. Have you been avoiding your hometown, or was it just me?"

"I was too busy to come back."

He nodded. "There was never enough for you here."

She clasped her hands together. "No. But the absence of pressure seems what I need right now. No reporters crawling through my windows."

"They didn't!"

Kate smiled sadly. "You do live in a small world," she observed. "That's not the half of it. But so far, I seem to have eluded the TV cameras by coming here."

"It's a shame it took a tragedy to bring you back. People around here feel slighted. They're proud of what you accomplished."

"I never meant to hurt anyone."

"I suppose I owe you an apology. I told you you were making a mistake by leaving."

She shook her head. "We both said a lot of ugly things we didn't mean at the end of that summer. I haven't come back to dredge up the past."

"Don't you think I know that? But this is a small town, and with your parents living across the street from mine, we can't help running into one another occasionally. Let's just close the lid on the past and try to salvage what's left of our friendship."

Kate nodded. In his own subtle way, he was forgiving her, even though she didn't deserve it.

He looked handsome and relaxed in his dark suit and pale-yellow shirt. When she noticed his tie, her lips curled into a smile. Playful puppies and kittens cavorted across the fabric.

"What?" he asked.

"Your tie," she told him, gesturing toward it with her head.

He laughed, lifting the tie and examining it. "I never leave my work at home. Mom gave me this. You know what a comedian she is."

"I know she's proud of you. Mom says you've got a clinic outside town."

"I'm in debt up to my eyebrows, but otherwise it's all mine."

"I'm glad you got what you wanted. You were always adopting stray animals. Remember the litter of pups we found behind the football stadium?"

"*You* found them. I only took them home."

"And found homes for all four of them."

"I had to. Mom threatened me. I don't know how many times she warned me, 'Grady, if you bring one more animal home . . . ' ''

Kate laughed. ''And then you hid that rooster in the garage without realizing it was going to start crowing at dawn.''

Grady chuckled. ''The whole block was up early that morning.''

Kate saw the boyish delight return to Grady's expression, and she realized how dangerously easy it would be to get swept back into a time that no longer existed. Especially now, when she was so vulnerable.

Grady stiffened suddenly, and she realized his thoughts must be echoing her own.

''It's good to see you again, Grady,'' she concluded abruptly.

He cast her a harsh glance. ''Are you really all right, Katie?'' he asked, his voice low.

A lump rose in her throat at hearing the familiar nickname from his lips. No one had called her Katie in a long, long time. She averted her gaze. She'd glimpsed pity and horror in too many eyes lately— and she couldn't bear to see it in his.

''I've heard you're spending all your time moping around your parents' house.''

Her eyes sparkled with ire. So, people were talking about her! He couldn't in light-years have begun to understand what she'd been through. ''Have you ever known me to mope?'' she challenged, cocking one eyebrow.

To her amazement, he met her defiance with a satisfied smirk.

''Still got the fight in you, I see,'' he concluded. ''As usual, you don't need anyone to worry about you. You look more beautiful than ever, by the way. And watch out for Noel. He's carrying a big torch for you.''

Kate gaped at Grady, her emotions raging. How dare he toy with her, make her argue with him, tell her she was beautiful. He'd always known how to infuriate her. He was as maddening as he was tender and gentle and honest and all the things she didn't want to remember.

''Don't be silly,'' she retorted.

''Did I hear my name?''

Kate shifted her glance to find Noel standing beside her, a glass of pop in one hand.

Grady patted Noel on the back. ''I don't see how anyone can hear anything above all this noise. I guess I'll be seeing where Libby's gone off to. I think Chandler may still have her captive. See you later, Katie.''

Baffled, Kate watched him walk off and reclaim his place at the petite woman's side. He was right, of course. She was a fighter. She would survive. But she'd never doubted that either. She just wanted to know when this icy feeling inside her would go away. When would she ever feel real again?

*   *   *

Snow continued falling through the night. Kate awoke Sunday morning feeling restless, unable to get her encounter with Grady out of her mind. Throwing back the comforter, she got up and went to the window of the upstairs bedroom, her old room in the house she'd grown up in. From here she looked out on the rooftops and treetops of Apple Blossom Drive, a street as sedate as its name implied. The road was lined with majestic, towering trees and stately older brick homes. Most of the residents were her parents' age or older, with the exception of a few younger professional couples attracted to this neighborhood for its character and charm.

No one was out this morning. The world was frosted with a perfect white glaze, silent and sparkling. The sky was clear now, a crystalline blue.

From here, she could see the Merediths' house two doors over across the street. Grady no longer lived there, but his three youngest brothers and sister still did. There were six Meredith siblings in all. Ordinarily, most of the traffic on this street was either bound to or coming from the Merediths' driveway.

She pulled her gaze from the window and shuffled to the closet for her corduroy robe. Although the big old house was centrally heated, the rooms stayed drafty in winter.

A week ago, she would have savored a day like today, the snow giving her a perfect excuse to stay inside. But this morning she felt as though she couldn't sit still.

Wrapped in her robe, she glanced around the room, remembering how it was once cluttered with travel posters and stuffed animals and school pennants. Her mother had cleared her things out of here long ago. Nothing remained but the furniture.

They'd given up on my ever coming home, she reflected guiltily. Sending them plane tickets to New York had always seemed easier than venturing back here.

Since her arrival, she'd set up her fax machine, her laptop computer, and her cellular phone. No matter how bad she felt, there was always company business needing her attention.

She couldn't help wondering whether she'd been making excuses to dodge Grady. Because deep inside, she'd known if she saw him again, it might not be so easy to keep convincing herself she was over him. Seeing him last night had evoked a sharp and mysterious sense of loss.

But she refused to make too much of that. Everything seemed magnified to her lately. Her emotions were as tender as a bruise.

Dropping down on the edge of the bed, she smiled wistfully, remembering how simple life had seemed during her sophomore year in high school. Grady, a senior, had developed a new attitude toward her. He'd noticed, finally, that she was a girl.

Of course, he'd known that all along, but he'd treated her like a pal while he dated girls in his own class. She supposed it was hard to view someone you'd grown up climbing trees and playing softball with in a romantic light. But that was the year he'd gotten around to asking her out.

He'd taken her to the state championship football game, and in the excitement when their team won, she'd leaped into his arms and been startled when he'd kissed her right there in the bleachers amid the scattered paper cups and waving pom-poms. No one was paying any attention to them, but he'd captured her attention completely.

She'd begun to doubt this would ever happen outside her dreams. They'd known each other most of their lives, but when he'd started high school, he grew strangely aloof. She'd hardly seen him except in passing. At the beginning of her freshman year, she was thrilled to finally be attending the same school he went to. Her heart dropped when he barely acknowledged her with a muttered "Hi" in the halls.

She'd nearly given up the next fall. Then he started walking home with her or driving her in the beat-up pickup Chandler McCorey had given him after he'd gotten it running again. Grady had worked for Mr. McCorey after school, delivering feed.

Suddenly she and Grady were friends again, as if the previous two years had never happened. She'd been happy enough for that. Then he'd asked her out.

She'd sometimes felt she'd burst with happiness and pride when he held her hand. She'd scrawled his name in ballpoint calligraphy on the margins of her notebooks. She envisioned the great future they'd have together. But that had been before she'd learned about making tough choices, about sacrificing one dream for another.

No one could ever know that her encounter with Grady last night had sparked a shadow of that old bubbly feeling inside her. It was a secret she'd keep to herself forever.

Folding her arms across her chest, she drifted back to the window. A familiar scraping sound drew her attention to Mr. Foley next door, who was shoveling his walk. He really was too old to be exerting himself so.

At first, she didn't pay much attention to the jade-green Explorer that pulled up to the curb across the street, a pony-sized gray dog looking eagerly out of one of the back windows. But when Grady, in a mustard-colored chesterfield, emerged from the driver's seat, her heart started tingling.

She watched with interest as he rounded the truck to open the passenger door. His companion from last night scooted out, the dog shooting past her, leaving a line of tracks in the snow. From here, she looked like Christmas Carol, bundled in a parka and matching red knit cap, scarf, and mittens. Grady reached out with one arm to catch the woman, who had tilted forward slightly and was laughing.

They seemed so happy and comfortable with each other, Kate noted. She'd never felt that way with anyone, except long ago, with Grady. Not, she told herself, that she was jealous. Grady was entitled to his happiness. And for the time being, she felt safer watching life go by from this distance.

Grady must be bringing his lady to Sunday dinner at his parents' house, a family ritual reserved for only those drawn close into the family circle.

Well, she certainly wasn't going to spend the day up here, mooning over old loves and keeping the Merediths' house under surveillance. Just because she'd never found room in her life for a serious relationship didn't mean Grady should be denied one. He deserved to be happy, and she wished that for him.

Backing away from the window, she decided to get dressed and give Mr. Foley a hand with his walk and maybe spare him from a heart attack. Then, her parents' drive needed clearing as well.

A few hours later, stiff, sore, and numb from cold, Kate surveyed her neighbor's cleared walkway and drive and her parents nearly cleared sidewalks with a tremendous sense of accomplishment. The sunny sky had clouded up again, and she feared more snow was coming.

Nothing like hard manual labor and bone-chilling

cold to clear your mind, she thought. At the moment she felt more exhilarated than she had after her one and only session with the high-priced trauma counselor the emergency room doctor had referred her to. The counselor was well qualified but had grated her nerves by talking down to her, as one would address a child who has skinned his knee. When the session was over, Kate had felt farther than ever from regaining her old sense of optimism, energy, and the belief she could accomplish anything she set out to do. Had all that been an illusion?

She brushed a shower of caked snow off her gloves. All things considered, she was glad to be nearly finished. She smiled, recalling her mother's shocked look when she'd marched downstairs bundled in jeans, an ancient sweater, boots, parka, gloves, knit cap, and scarf, announcing her plans. Now she realized she'd done little since she'd come home except vegetate in her room.

But out here in this silent world, she felt as though she were alone on some strange planet. And that was all right with her. No one expected anything of her.

When she'd first come out and urged Mr. Foley to go back inside and cozy up with a second cup of coffee and the Sunday paper, he'd stared at her as though a lunatic had accosted him. Mr. Foley had a long-standing reputation around the neighborhood as an old grouch. With his round bald head, leathery complexion, and constant frown, he resembled a jack-o'-

lantern. One glare out his window had always been enough to send kids out playing scattering away from his house.

As a child, Kate had been terrified of him, until she realized he looked meaner than he actually was. Kate realized she'd been hiding inside the house so long, her appearance must have seemed to him like a ghost materializing. She'd become the Boo Radley of Shady Pointe—not exactly her goal in life.

"I need the fresh air," she'd assured him, gesturing toward his house. "Go on. I'll finish this."

He'd studied her and then simply said, "God bless you." Kate had pushed down an unexpected lump in her throat. She'd kept her emotions so rigidly controlled these past few months, his outburst of sentiment grated her in places she'd been keeping well protected.

Now, just a few more scoops and she could go inside to thaw out and get something to eat. Her growling stomach reminded her she'd bypassed breakfast. The smell of cooking was in the air, and she suspected it was coming from the Merediths' house.

As she dug the shovel into the snow, she felt a presence behind her.

Whipping around, she found herself face-to-face with the monstrous dog she'd seen bound out of Grady's vehicle earlier. Up close, he was even bigger than he'd looked from upstairs. And he was unaccompanied by Grady or anyone else.

"Shoo!" she commanded with a wave of her arm.

The beast cocked his head, not backing away.

With a heavy sigh, she decided he might go away if she ignored him. She was more annoyed than afraid. Grady wouldn't have owned a mean dog.

Turning her back to him, she resumed shoveling snow. What was wrong with Grady? He knew better than to let a dog run loose.

A low growl from behind her caused her to freeze in her boot prints. When she turned, the goofy-looking dog was poised to attack. Arching low, he dared her to move.

Fear speared her now.

"Go home!" she hollered angrily.

He stared at her with dull, defiant eyes.

Well, she'd had enough. Even if it meant confronting Grady, she was going across the street to tell him to come and get his dog or moose or whatever this was.

As she took a step forward, the dog lunged forward, batting a huge paw at her.

"Scram!" she screamed, truly alarmed when she saw the dog wasn't about to let her pass.

She clutched the handle of the snow shovel tightly. She knew she couldn't bring herself to smash the animal's head with it, but she could hold him back.

Everything happened at once. The front door opened, her father filling the door frame. Mr. Foley emerged from his side door, moving at a speed incredible for his age, and pointing a shotgun at the dog's head.

Kate's stomach rolled and her breath caught as she realized what was about to happen. Mr. Foley was going to kill this dog right at her feet.

"No!" she screamed, surprised to hear another voice echo her cry.

She looked across the street, where Grady, without benefit of coat or hat, stood on the curb, a look of utter horror on his face.

Mr. Foley eased the shotgun down. Grady rushed across the pavement.

"Put that thing away, James," Kate's dad snapped from the front porch.

"Come here, Ollie," Grady ordered as he approached.

The dog, unaware of impending danger, lumbered happily to its owner. Grady caught hold of his collar.

At the thought of what had nearly occurred, Kate felt the blood drain from her head. Her knees were shaking, her stomach queasy.

"Are you all right?" Grady asked, watching her suddenly go pale.

Kate nodded.

"I'm sorry about Ollie," Grady apologized. "He's just a puppy, and he was trying to play with you. He was in the yard, and I guess he must have jumped the fence."

Kate was trying to find the words to tell Grady no

harm was done. But her lips seemed glued. All she could think about was the violence she had nearly been responsible for. She should have been able to handle the dog. She never would have forgiven herself had Mr. Foley pulled the trigger in her defense.

"Go on inside, Kate," Norman Smithers instructed. Confused and feeling like a two-year-old, she headed toward the house.

As she walked away, she heard her father chewing Grady out for allowing his dog to roam loose. Grady, who she knew would apologize if he was wrong, but never more than once, began raising his voice, asking why Mr. Foley was running around the neighborhood toting an Uzi.

"It wasn't an Uzi," she heard Norman counter.

As the voices behind her rose, Kate turned. "It was an accident," she implored, her hands clenched in fists. "Let's all forget it, please."

The two men fell silent, directing their glances to her.

"No harm was done. The dog startled me, and I overreacted. I'm just glad he wasn't hurt," she said. Without waiting for a response, she turned and disappeared into the house.

Chapter Three

All the bright lights and shiny tinsel at Christmas-
time served only to emphasize the hollowness behind
the gaiety, Kate reflected. How absurd human beings
were to once a year pretend their lives were in order,
that their actions were motivated by charity toward
others. Then in the gray light of the year's final days,
they were shaken to find nothing has changed.

Maybe Christmas shopping this afternoon hadn't
been such a good idea after all. Kate pushed the neg-
ative thoughts from her mind as she made her way
through the aisles of Vine's Department Store. She'd
hoped the outing might restore her spirits.

She tried not to think about this being her first time
out alone since she'd come home. After all, she'd vis-

ited downtown Shady Pointe a thousand times, shopped in this store ever since she was old enough to have her own money. Coming here this afternoon was no big deal, she told herself.

And if she ever wanted her life to go back to normal, she had to start doing things for herself once again. She couldn't hide away forever.

She stood back, trying to work up admiration for a set of china edged in gold and decorated with holly sprigs. Would her mother like it? Reaching out, she flipped one of the cups and found the price tag, wincing as she read it. While she could well afford to splurge, she hesitated to pay this much for something she wasn't sure her mom wanted. Her parents stood so consistently behind her; she wanted gifts for them sufficient to express her gratitude.

She realized she'd nearly bought the china simply to hasten her shopping. It wasn't like her to settle for less than what she wanted. What you accept is what you end up with, her Grandmother Smithers always used to tell her. When had it become so difficult for her to make even the simplest decision?

Shaking her head, she glanced down the aisle. Most residents of Shady Pointe were still at work on this Thursday afternoon, so despite the season, the store wasn't crowded. Harp music played over the loudspeakers, and the pillars were wrapped with tinsel garlands. As a young girl, she'd come here tingling with anticipation of selecting gifts with the few dollars she'd saved from her allowance.

Now she could afford just about anything in the store, but the joy was gone. This was simply a chore, no more exciting than peeling potatoes or doing laundry.

She smiled as she thought of her mother. Convincing Julia she didn't have to accompany her on this outing had been like wrestling a lion. She'd looked stunned, then worried, when Kate had announced her plans over lunch.

"Alone?" Julia had asked. "I'll be happy to go with you."

"And miss your club meeting this afternoon?" Kate had asked. "I want to go by myself, Mom. Besides, how can I buy your present if you're standing right there?"

At that, Julia had launched into a lecture on why it wasn't necessary to buy her anything.

"Just having you here is enough," Julia had insisted. "When I think of nearly—"

"Don't." Kate had cut her off. She didn't want to think about the accident today, didn't want anything to grate at her resolve.

Seeing Grady last weekend had shaken her into action. Somehow, it had hurt more than anything to have him view her as a weakling.

Now, she glanced down the far end of the aisle,

astonished to see Grady himself had materialized. He stood there scanning a display.

Blanching as if she'd seen a ghost, she quickly turned away, pretending not to have noticed him.

But it was too late. He was already heading in her direction.

"Katie!" he called to her.

Ignoring him was impossible.

She turned back, feigning surprise. She was a poor actress, and her attempt at deception made her uncomfortable.

"Grady," she greeted him. "I'm surprised to see you here. Who's tending the animals?"

"We close the clinic early on Thursdays. Compensates for working Saturdays. I was hoping to get my Christmas shopping over with, but I'm feeling a little overwhelmed." He extended empty arms. "As you can see, I'm not exactly loaded down with packages."

She nodded, then pointed to the china. "I was considering this for Mom, but I don't think she'd use it."

Grady spotted a price tag and gave a low whistle.

Kate tossed back the mane of long hair she'd worn down today and offered a faint smile of agreement. "You're right. It *is* overpriced. And there doesn't seem to be the selection here I remember. I think I'll check out the antiques store down the street. I've been dy . . . anxious to check it out." Stumbling upon an excuse to leave Vine's was sheer inspiration.

"Mind if I tag along?" he asked as easily as he

might have commented on the weather. "On my own, I don't know an antique from an antelope. Maybe you could advise me."

Kate tensed. She'd assumed he was hunting a gift for his girlfriend. Surely Grady wouldn't be so indelicate as to ask her to help pick something out.

She shrugged noncommitally. "I'm no expert," she qualified. "But you're welcome to come."

He grinned. "You realize Mrs. Ziffretti will think this is her lucky day when you walk in."

"Mrs. Ziffretti owns the store?" she asked incredulously. "The same Mrs. Ziffretti who made American history the most boring subject in high school?"

"You got it. She finally retired, then opened the shop to have something to do."

"She must be about a hundred years old by now."

"Actually, I think she's in her early seventies."

Kate remembered Mrs. Ziffretti as a well-meaning person who'd been severely out of touch with her students and who lectured in a low monotone Kate had always had to strain to hear.

"You've gotten me curious to see her now," Kate reported. "I don't see any point in lingering here."

"I'm ready to go," he reported.

Grady fell in step beside her, and Kate felt stiff in his presence, although he was acting as though there was nothing unusual about their shopping together.

"Do you remember the Christmas we made candles for everyone?" she asked suddenly, coloring slightly at her impulsive statement. It had been their last Christmas together, her senior year. He'd been home on break from college.

"My mom claims she's still scraping wax off the kitchen walls," he said, seeming to find nothing unsettling in the memory.

"That's the last time Christmas even really felt like Christmas."

"That's because you were still a kid. Christmas is for kids."

"Still, I'd like to feel some kind of wonder . . ." she said wistfully.

"It comes back when I watch my nieces and nephews," he told her. "But think of how many little girls are looking forward to getting Calico Crissie dolls this year."

"Designing Crissie wasn't the accomplishment people make it out to be. She's been in my head ever since I was a little girl. I just make the kind of doll I'd always wanted."

"You shouldn't make light of it. Few people would have had the gumption to go out and make a wild dream a reality."

No matter what the cost, Kate reflected, walking beneath the arc of his arm as they reached the front door and he opened it for her.

She stepped onto Maple Street, the town's main thoroughfare. A Salvation Army Santa, too thin to look realistic, sat ringing his bell. The light poles were wrapped with ropes of fake evergreen, huge wreaths dangling at the tops. Fat, dark clouds overhead made it look later than it was, and the wreaths were dancing in the wind. Kate wondered if it were going to snow again. The accumulation from the weekend had begun to melt, then had crusted over with an icy glaze as temperatures fell below freezing again and stayed there.

Shady Pointe's downtown business area was a far cry from Manhattan. About three blocks long, it sported the usual post office, bank, and drugstore. Aside from Vine's, the antiques store and a few clothing stores, there weren't many places to shop. Kate knew her parents and most of their friends postponed their shopping for out-of-town trips to malls and major department stores. But she wanted to spend her money here. She owed at least that to a place that had shaped her life in more ways than she'd realized.

Walking behind her, Grady planted a hand on the back of her coat as he guided her through the traffic on the sidewalk.

When they were past the entrance to Vine's, he let his hand drop and drew alongside her.

"I'm glad I ran into you, Katie. I wanted you to know I've given Ollie a stern lecture about his behavior Sunday. I'm afraid mine wasn't exactly sterling either."

"A leash might be more effective."

"For him or for me?"

Without answering, she cast him a sly, sidelong glance.

"It's a little embarrassing for someone who makes a living dealing with animals to own such a wild beast, isn't it? I'm trying to train him. First dog I've ever had trouble with," Grady admitted.

"Why keep him?" she asked.

"Nobody else wants him. Normally I've been able to find homes for most of the strays I pick up. But Ollie's big, awkward, and ugly. I guess I'm stuck with him. Besides, I kind of like him. I admire his spirit."

Kate laughed lightly.

"Orneriness, don't you mean?" she asked. Grady wasn't one to back down from a challenge. Kate fully believed he'd make Ollie the best-behaved dog in the county.

"I suppose it depends on how you look at it."

"Ollie wasn't the only one out of line. Dad and Mr. Foley mistakenly thought I need their protection."

"Imagine that. Here we are," he noted, stopping short in front of Glass & Lace. The display widows, lined with miniature Christmas lights, boasted an intriguing assortment of blown-glass ornaments and old Santa figures strewn amongst doilies, goblets, and miscellaneous items including a manual typewriter and a well pump.

"That display never changes," he informed her after catching her inspecting it. "Mrs. Ziffretti just adds seasonal touches to it." He pulled open the door and bells jingled overhead.

The shop's interior was dark but warm. Kate smelled a gas heater burning, and the musty scent of long-stored belongings was masked by cinnamon and apple potpourri.

She felt Grady come in behind her and heard the bells as the door swung shut. It took a moment for her eyes to adjust to the dim light.

"Can I help you, ma'am?" a voice cut through the darkness. "Why, Dr. Meredith—you're the last person I ever expected to see in here."

"Anything can happen this time of year." He ushered Kate closer to the counter. "You remember Katie Smithers, don't you, Mrs. Ziffretti?"

Kate heard the astonished gasp as a long, thin form bowed over the counter.

Mrs. Ziffretti's thin lips formed an O, and she clasped spindly fingers to her cheeks. "Why, you still look the same, child. You always were such a beautiful, intelligent girl," she assessed.

Kate's skin heated under such lavish praise. She felt guilty for not having remembered her former teacher more fondly.

"And I'd heard you'd suffered horrible burns."

Katie tensed.

"She wasn't burned," Grady explained quietly.

"I'm perfectly fine, Mrs. Ziffretti," Katie added,

unwilling to sit back and allow Grady to speak for her. "I wasn't injured in the accident."

Mrs. Ziffretti's gray brow knit over her long, narrow face. "But I thought . . ."

Katie glimpsed the warning expression Grady was giving her.

"In any case, it's wonderful to have you back."

"I don't mean to be rude," Kate explained. "But I don't like talking about the accident."

Mrs. Ziffretti patted her hand. "Of course not. But you're among friends here."

"I was wondering, could you help me pick out something for my mother?" Katie cut her off.

A slow smile overtook the woman's perplexed expression, and Kate remembered what Grady had predicted.

"Certainly, dear, tell me what you have in mind. When you're finished shopping, I have hot chocolate in the back room . . . for special customers."

As Mrs. Ziffretti led her through the shop, a hodgepodge of genuine treasures mixed in with junk that wasn't even really old, leftovers from someone's garage sale no doubt, Katie's admiration for the woman grew. Here, she was in her element more than she had ever been as a teacher.

She came out from around the glass counter, and Kate was startled to see her dressed in jeans and a cable-knit sweater, a far cry from the old-fashioned long dresses and pumps she'd worn to school.

"Did you have something particular in mind?" she asked.

"Not really," Kate replied. "But I'll know it when I see it."

"Take your time and look around then. There's a story behind every item in here."

She went back to the counter, where she was working a crossword puzzle. Kate wondered how she could read in this dim light.

Following the older woman's advice, Kate took her time browsing. Grady drifted off to the other side of the shop. Once, she noticed him picking up a green glass vase, the kind used routinely in any flower shop, and inspecting it with interest. Catching his eye, she shook her head, and he quickly set it down.

Kate smiled to herself as she returned her attention to the merchandise, hoping to locate some misplaced treasure. Were she a mean-spirited person, she might have encouraged him to buy the vase. She could imagine the look on his friend's face as she unwrapped it, groping for flattering words that wouldn't betray what she really thought of it.

Kate was reaching for a blue glass candy dish that had drawn her attention when she spotted the brooch, nearly buried beneath the other junk. Without thinking, she gasped. And she'd been to enough country auctions to know better than to betray excitement. She'd noticed that none of Mrs. Ziffretti's merchandise was marked, and she knew she'd just push up the price.

But the brooch was too intriguing to be ignored. Just old costume jewelry really, it was shaped like a peacock and studded with multicolored rhinestones. The metal was tarnished, but none of the stones was missing.

She captured it in the palm of her hand and raised it to her face for closer inspection. Her mother would never wear this, she reasoned, and she had no one else to buy it for. Still, she'd taken a liking to it and a few months ago, she would have bought it to set off her red pullover.

At the moment, buying it for herself just didn't feel right. Maybe she'd think about it and come back.

As she moved to put it back, Grady, standing over her shoulder, halted her movement by capturing her wrist.

"Pretty," he said. "Are you going to buy it?"

"No," Kate replied.

He swung his glance toward Mrs. Ziffretti, and the heat of him standing so near, his strong hold on her slender wrist, unsettled Kate.

"How much is this brooch, Mrs. Ziffretti?" he inquired.

She named a reasonable price.

He turned back to her. Kate feared he was about to ask her opinion on whether his friend might like it.

"Are you sure you don't want it?" he asked instead. Apparently, her reaction to it had escaped Mrs. Ziffretti but not Grady.

"Yes, I'm sure."

He scooped it into his larger hand. "I'll take it then," he announced.

Kate's spirits deflated. She didn't need to ask what he was going to do with it. In the heart of her, she knew it wasn't going to his mom or his sisters. It wasn't valuable, but it was unusual, and she'd taken a liking to it. Why hadn't she bought it? Oh, well, she couldn't very well change her mind now.

Grady paid for the brooch and Kate, feeling obligated not to leave the store empty-handed, purchased the candy dish for her mother.

Mrs. Ziffretti insisted they join her in the back room for hot chocolate, a watery concoction she served in chipped china cups.

"Don't you need to stay up front?" Kate asked.

"That's what the bell is for," Mrs. Ziffretti informed her. "Besides, I don't get many customers." She shook her head. "Have you heard, Grady, that Vine's is closing down after the first of the year?"

Both Grady and Kate flashed shocked looks.

Grady rubbed his clean-shaven, angular jaw. "No," he answered, "I hadn't heard that."

"Well, none of us is going to last too long once Vine's is gone," she predicted with resignation. "This is going to turn into a ghost town."

"Why is Vine's closing?" Grady asked.

"Phil's been wanting to retire for years. I guess he'd hoped one of his kids would take it over one day, but one of his sons is a lawyer and the other's a stockbroker and they've both moved off. His daughter opened a gift shop in Chicago after she got married, and I hear she's doing well. She was his last hope, I think. He's had the place for sale for years, quietly, you know, but no takers."

"If he could just stick it out a while longer . . . this town is bound to bounce back."

"I don't think Phil's going to wait any longer. You know his wife died when the kids were still small and he raised them alone. Last summer, he took a cruise and met a woman he wants to marry. Only problem is she's ten years younger than he is and operates a ranch in west Texas. She's not about to give that up to come to Shady Pointe, and the way things are going here, I don't blame them."

Kate had never heard Mrs. Ziffretti's voice punctuated by so much emotion before.

"She owns a ranch?"

"She and her husband ran it before he died." Mrs. Ziffretti clasped her hands together and looped them around one knee. "Women today have so much opportunity. Like you, Kate. In my day, a woman didn't think about starting a business. She was either a teacher or a nurse or she got married and raised a family."

Avoiding Grady's eyes, Kate flinched inwardly.

"Maybe someone will at least rent Vine's building and move something else in," she speculated.

Mrs. Ziffretti shook her head. "Shady Pointe's finished. I don't mind so much for myself—I've had my chance. I suppose I'll still be able to hang on for a while; this shop doesn't pull in much income anyway, and I've got my pension. But it's a shame for the younger people. This used to be such a nice place to live. We had community fairs and dances on the weekends, and folks pitched in to help one another out."

"The world changes," Kate noted.

"It's a shame that developer isn't going to get his chance to build over at Echo Lake. The way I see it, attracting some summer people might hold this town together," Mrs. Ziffretti said firmly.

Grady's head snapped up. "How did you know about that?" he asked.

"One advantage of maintaining a shop down here is you learn what's going on. I've heard rumblings about your running for mayor as well."

Grady waved her off. "Not from me, you haven't."

Mrs. Ziffretti smiled. "Don't you realize, Grady, you're one of the people with the most at stake? With your clinic here, you can't up and leave. You'd better join Hewett and his cronies or do something about him."

His eyes narrowed. "I'm not teaming up with . . . Hewett. I despise the way he operates. But I have no intention of running for office."

"In any case—" Mrs. Ziffretti swept her gaze dramatically over the two of them. "—it is good to see the two of you back together again."

At their red, astonished faces, she raised an amused eyebrow. "You didn't think I noticed what went on in the halls and who was dating whom back then, did you?" she asked.

"We met up by chance this afternoon," Kate explained quickly. She wouldn't have felt compelled to do so except she didn't want Mrs. Ziffretti spreading rumors that they were seeing each other again. She didn't care what people might say about her, but she certainly didn't want something so innocent to come between Grady and his friend.

Mrs. Ziffretti nodded, looking unconvinced. "Too bad," she lamented. "And both of you have done so well for yourselves. You both had that spark back in school. A teacher learns to sense which of her students are going to make it."

Fortunately, the bell over the door clattered, announcing the arrival of another customer.

Kate took the cue. "I've got to be going," she announced, rising.

"Come back again, Grady. And you too, Kate," Mrs. Ziffretti urged as she rose. "I didn't mean to be crude earlier. I was just so relieved to see how well you're doing . . ."

Kate dismissed the apology with a wave. "Thank you. I've enjoyed our visit."

From the front of the store, Mrs. Ziffretti gasped. Kate and Grady exchanged anxious glances.

"For goodness' sake!" Mrs. Ziffretti's voice drifted to the back. "It's snowing again."

Chapter Four

Kate had had to hold on to her flying hair as she walked out into a whirlwind of snowflakes. The air was hard and brittle, smelling of snow.

She looked up at Grady, who stood behind her.

"I'd better get home," she told him.

"Don't rush off," he countered, leaning close to be heard over the wind. "Mrs. Ziffretti whetted my taste for some real hot chocolate—the kind with a mountain of whipped cream on top."

"Nobody serves that anymore," Kate argued.

"You're on," he said, and to her chagrin, she realized she'd inadvertently agreed to accompany him.

She kept up with his long strides.

"My mother didn't call you, did she?" she asked suspiciously.

"Was she supposed to?"

"Now that I recall, she was extremely reluctant to let me go into town without a baby-sitter."

She wasn't going to add that Julia had always believed her daughter made a mistake by not marrying Grady, and would have jumped at any opportunity to throw them together, even now.

Grady appraised her evenly. "I wished to express my appreciation for your saving me from buying that vase. It was plain, wasn't it?"

She laughed. "You can get them by the dozens for about a dime apiece at any garage sale."

"You're a tough negotiator, aren't you?" he asked. "But then you always were."

Kate didn't answer him. No matter what direction their conversation took, it always seemed to curve full circle into the past.

A short while later, Grady was stretching his long frame back in a booth inside the Sandwich Works, watching Katie whittle down the mound of whipped cream with the edge of her spoon, something he must have seen her do a thousand times. The windowpane beside him was frosted with cold, snowflakes sticking to the glass.

"You certainly made a point of letting Mrs. Ziffretti know we'd come there together only by accident," he said suddenly.

She looked up. "I know how people here like to talk. I don't want to cause any problems for you."

For a moment he looked puzzled. Then his expression hardened. "With Libby, you mean?"

"Your date the other night."

"That's Libby. I appreciate your concern, Kate, but Libby knows you and I are old friends. She knows the rest of it ended long ago." He raised his eyebrows. "We *are* still friends, aren't we?"

Kate nodded tentatively, then her eyes dropped to her cocoa, as if she expected to read her fortune in it. His casual dismissal of their old relationship wasn't a surprise, of course, yet it sounded so final and flat. She waited to hear more, but he'd stopped talking. She realized she'd foolishly and unrealistically been hoping he'd qualify his relationship with Libby, tell her it wasn't serious. But he didn't.

She dipped the end of her spoon into the steaming cocoa. "I wonder how many square feet are in the Vine's building?" she pondered, anxious to change the subject.

"You two all set?" Katie looked up to see the proprietor standing over them, grinning. He was a slim, appealing-looking young man with dark hair, olive skin, and a broad smile. He couldn't have been much older than Noel.

"Fine, thanks, Benny," Grady replied. When Benny didn't retreat, he added reluctantly, "Do you know Kate Smithers?"

Benny turned his shining smile on her and extended his hand. "You probably don't remember me," he said. "But I've heard of you, and I'm impressed."

Kate shook his hand, ignoring his overt flattery. "You've done wonders with this place," Kate complimented him, sweeping a hand to indicate the bright lights, checkerboard linoleum, ice cream parlor tables and chairs in the area between the booths, and a replica of an old-fashioned soda fountain. A restored jukebox, its multicolored lights glowing, sat against the far wall. "I remember it as a decrepit old diner."

"It was, thanks," Benny agreed. "I've tried to keep the old favorites on the menu while revamping the atmosphere. Grady, don't forget the Christmas dance at the club tomorrow night. You're welcome to come as my guest, Kate."

"I have another commitment," Grady said quickly.

Benny looked absolutely insulted, and Kate got the idea this was not the first time Grady had turned down an invitation from him.

"I'm afraid I do as well," she added. "But thank you."

"What was that all about?" she asked after he was gone.

Grady shrugged it off. "Politics," he answered.

"More pressure to run for mayor?" she asked.

"Hardly." He lowered his voice. "Not from Hewett's grandson anyway."

Kate raised one hand to her open mouth. "I didn't

stop to make the connection. Why don't you want to run, anyway? As I remember, you were president of your senior class and did a terrific job.''

He stared into the far corner of the room. ''I would have expected you to be the last person to encourage me to let what other people want dictate my life.''

''But Grady, you love this town.''

''I was born here, just like you were. My staying here doesn't necessarily indicate affection.''

She looked at the untouched mug on the table before him. ''Your cocoa is getting cold,'' she reminded him.

Grady stirred the whipped cream until it dissolved into the cocoa, then raised the steaming cup to his lips. But Katie held his interest more than the beverage. From outward appearances, she didn't look as though anything out of the ordinary had happened to her. But he saw through her facade and knew her ordeal had affected her deeply. As usual, she was brave. He remembered when, as kids, she'd fallen out of the crab apple tree in his yard, bruising herself badly. Refusing assistance, she'd hobbled across the street to her house, her eyelashes fluttering and her teeth pressed into her bottom lip as she struggled to keep from crying. He could only imagine the horror she'd lived through with the accident, and he ached for her. They'd grown up together, and he told himself the lingering fondness he felt was only natural. He wished he could comfort her, but he feared she would push him away, as she'd done when he tried to help her up after she'd fallen out of the tree.

He'd been remembering that incident ever since she'd refused to buy the brooch at Mrs. Ziffretti's, even though she'd obviously been taken with it. He'd seen it in her eyes. Why had she declined giving in to that small impulse? Moreover, he wondered now why he had bought it. Maybe so she'd know where to find it when she changed her mind.

Odd, with his knack for talking to and calming wounded animals, he wasn't sure where to start with a human being.

With her loose hair hanging around her shoulders, she looked almost like the young girl he remembered. Unaware he was watching her, she wore a relaxed expression. He'd nearly missed recognizing her earlier; she was dressed so casually, her jeans tucked into knee-high leather boots, with a pale blue mohair sweater and a white parka with faux fur lining the hood.

A twinge of guilt struck him. Julia Smithers hadn't called and asked him to escort Katie this afternoon, as Kate accused. But then, she'd been quick to tell him where Katie was when he'd called. He'd thought this might be a good chance to settle the unfinished business between them.

He finished the last of the cocoa in silence.

Katie cast a worried glance out the window. ''The

snow's coming down harder,'' she observed. ''I really do need to get home.''

''Where are you parked?'' he asked.

''In the lot behind Vine's,'' she replied.

''I'll walk you to your car.''

''You don't have to.''

''I know I don't have to.''

She reached for her pocketbook, and he waved a hand in protest. ''My treat,'' he insisted.

For a moment, she looked as though she were going to argue, then she didn't. ''Thanks,'' she said.

She went on outside as he paid their bill. He caught up to her on the sidewalk. Snow was falling fast and furious, clinging to her hair and eyelashes.

He reached out and pulled her hood over her head. ''I can't believe we're getting this much snow before Christmas,'' he noted as he tucked his hands in his coat pocket and ducked against the wind.

''It's beautiful,'' she commented. ''I've always liked the snow. Nothing else transforms the world so completely. It's almost magical.''

Grady, walking beside her, leaned sideways. ''You won't be thinking magical when you're shoveling the driveway again,'' he countered.

She'd seemed to snap back to life out here. Some of the light had come back into her eyes, and her complexion glowed.

''You know,'' she said, ''I really don't understand what's happening in this town. Benny's sandwich shop is so uptown and modern, and everything else I've seen is falling apart. It doesn't seem to fit in.''

Grady shrugged. ''A few other places are doing well, for now—those run by our mayor and his sup- porters. They don't seem to understand their success depends on everyone being able to make a living here. More and more people are finding jobs elsewhere and moving away. I'm afraid if Vine's closes, it will be the end of this town.''

''Is that why you don't like Benny?''

''I like him fine. I just don't want to be recruited into Hewett Sparks' little clique. My clinic's outside the city limits, so they can't pressure me. Maybe there's nothing I can do to stop them, but I don't have to join them.''

''As mayor you could stop them.''

''Katie, I'm not sure there's even enough of this town left to save. Things have been running Hewett's way for decades. But his buddies are dying out, retir- ing, and no one's taking over. Sure, it makes me mad. My life's all wrapped up in this place, my business, my family. But I don't have time to run a political campaign. Why are you interested in the Vine's build- ing?''

''I have an idea. My toy company's been looking for a location for an outlet store.''

''Here? In Shady Pointe?''

''If there's a development coming in . . .''

He shook his head. ''Don't bank on that. And be

careful who you mention anything about it to. Are you planning on staying here?''

He wasn't sure why that prospect disturbed him so. He'd assumed she'd be heading back to New York after the holidays. And he'd been fully prepared to deal with her on those terms—this time.

''No.'' She avoided his glance. ''I couldn't.''

Only after she said it did he recognize his disappointment. Foolish, either way; they weren't part of each other's lives anymore. And Shady Pointe was even duller now than it had been when she left. Why should it hold any appeal for her now? After New York, this place must seem drearier than ever.

''You know, Katie, I know you better than most people. You blame yourself when anything goes wrong. And, believe me, nobody can endure that kind of responsibility. When Kevin got sick, I thought it was my fault because I'd envied the attention he got as the baby of the family. And my parents thought it was because of something they'd done. But what it boils down to is bad things happen—fires, earthquakes, planes falling out of the sky. No single person can foresee or prevent these things.''

''No. Your brother's illness wasn't your fault,'' she stated flatly.

The storm had driven most of the holiday shoppers away. Only a few scattered cars remained in the lot.

''My car's practically buried already,'' she announced as they slid around the corner of the brick building that housed Vine's. She pointed to a rose-colored BMW.

Grady looked down into eyes sparkling like gilded china. Snowflakes laced the reddish hair jutting out from beneath her hood, framing her face like a mantilla. He saw pain in her eyes, but she refused to acknowledge it, let alone allow anyone to help ease it.

A sudden wrenching in his chest reminded him how much he'd once loved her. He squelched his sudden impulse to kiss her, attributing it to nostalgia. After all, they'd been kids together, enjoying easier times. It seemed to him he'd passed thirty overnight, and Katie was nearing that age. The instinct to try to turn back the clock, recapture lost youth, was tempting.

But you could never really go back. To try to do so would be a grave mistake. All he wanted to do was cheer her up.

Forcing his eyes away from her, he looked across the expanse of concrete, where fresh snow topped the hard-packed remnants of the earlier storm.

He glanced furtively in all directions to be sure no one was watching. ''Remember this?'' he asked, back-pedaling to get a running start, then sliding several feet along the concrete. He wondered if anyone who saw him now would be urging him to run for mayor.

But the effort was worthwhile when he heard Katie's delighted, bubbly laugh.

''I haven't surfed on ice in an eternity,'' she said,

wearing a devilish expression as she worked into her own running start.

Too eager, she pushed too hard and took off too abruptly, flying across the slick ice and wobbling as her boots threatened to shoot out from under her. Her hands flailed wildly. A shattering sounded as her package slipped from her hand.

Grady rushed up and caught her by the waist.

"Careful," he murmured, meaning to pull her upright, but inadvertently drawing him against her instead. In her panic, she leaned into him, grasping his arms.

He looked down at her to ask if she was all right. Her face, inches below his, was red from cold and excitement and damp from melted snow. Her eyes were wide and expectant, a faint smile curling her lips. Her expression conveyed surprise, amusement, and something else he couldn't read.

"Your package," he said.

"Never mind. It wasn't anything I really wanted."

Forgetting everything else, for the snow-cloaked world seemed as private as a distant planet, he lowered his mouth to her upraised lips.

His intended kiss fell short as Katie suddenly tensed and jumped backward.

He opened his eyes, searching for an explanation, to find her wide-eyed and pointing across the street.

Puzzled and annoyed, he turned in the direction she was pointing.

Increasingly perplexed, he turned back to her.

"Did you see him?" she asked anxiously.

"Who?"

"There was a man across the street, standing there, watching us."

Grady drew in a sharp breath. If she had wanted to avoid what almost happened, she didn't need to invent imaginary diversions.

"For Pete's sake, Katie. I didn't see anybody."

"He was standing right there." She pointed emphatically. "And he must have scurried off when you turned around."

Grady realized what nearly happened shouldn't have happened. And he could see Katie believed someone had been there. For a second, he'd forgotten how fragile she was.

"Probably just someone passing by on his way to the store. You were quite a comical sight, dancing around on the ice."

"I hope he was just some casual observer," she said, turning up her collar.

He eyed her with concern. "What do you mean?"

"I'd hate to think the press had found me."

He hadn't considered that possibility.

He lowered one eyebrow. "Do you really think a reporter would come this far to find you?"

Slowly, she nodded. "A certain kind of reporter might." She clenched her fists in fury at the prospect her privacy had been invaded. "I'm sure you don't keep up with tabloid journalism, but unfortunately, a few weeks before the accident I was photographed at a restaurant with Hall Dunwood. Speculation created by that incident fueled the press's interest in me.''

Grady gave a low whistle. She didn't like the way he was studying her.

''Hall Dunwood . . . the movie actor?''

''Yes.''

She realized Grady, like everyone else, was jumping to the wrong conclusions and began to explain, but he abruptly dropped the subject. ''Let's dig your car out. I'm parked back out on the street. You can warm up your engine while I pull around.''

''Why?'' she asked.

''I'll follow you home. Just in case someone else is following you.''

''I don't want to cause any trouble.''

''You've been away a long time. People around here help one another out, remember? Despite Mrs. Ziffretti's voice of doom, that's one thing that hasn't changed.''

''Thanks, Grady.''

He swept the snow off her roof with a single pass of his long arm.

A few minutes later, Kate was sitting in her car with the engine idling, thawing her hands in the stream of warm air from the heating vent.

Grady was probably right. The man she had seen most likely had merely been passing by. Maybe she was overly sensitive about escaping media attention, but she'd experienced the callousness of eager reporters who balked at nothing. One had entered the emergency room while she was lying dazed on a stretcher.

"What did it feel like when the plane went down? When did you realize Harold Young was dead?" he'd asked, sticking a microphone in her face.

Until that moment, she hadn't been sure Harold had been killed.

No, she wasn't talking to the press. Her distress, her grief, were no one's business but her own.

Her heart was still racing, her stomach trembling from what had nearly happened before she'd spotted the man across the street. Grady had been about to kiss her, and she'd wanted him to. How deeply she'd needed that small comfort. All those old feelings couldn't possibly have survived the time, the separation, the hurt. No, nothing more than a deep-rooted curiosity had thrown them together. Grady probably, like her, had wondered if it would feel the same, if any of the magic remained.

His kisses always had been magical, she recalled, remembering them more vividly than she wanted to. She was glad they'd been interrupted. If she had any feelings left for Grady, she couldn't deal with having them resurface now. And she didn't want to be responsible for the guilt he'd feel over betraying Libby. He'd taken his girlfriend to his parents' house for dinner—he *had* to be serious about her. No, she'd been acting selfishly.

Briefly, she considered taking off before Grady returned. But before she had a chance to decide, his Explorer rolled around the corner.

She waited for him to pull up behind her, then eased out of the lot.

He stayed behind her all the way to her parents' house, stopping while she pulled into the drive, then taking off with a brief honk and a wave.

There were no other cars behind him.

"I'm glad you decided to come to this sledding party," Noel told Kate as he navigated his Blazer over the winding, snow-covered back roads in the darkness.

"It sounds like fun," Kate replied from the passenger seat, straining to see through the window into the darkness. "But where are we?" Actually, she'd jumped at Noel's invitation. He was the only person around here who treated her the same way he always had. And with him, she had hopes of feeling she was okay. She felt as safe and comfortable as she would have with a younger brother, if she'd had one.

"We're almost there," he assured her. "Do you remember Chelsea Bartlett? We're going to her parents' farm."

Kate shook her head. "I don't think I know her."

"She was a year behind me in school. Teaches kindergarten now."

66
Jan McDaniel

"I think I remember her parents. They have the huge hill. Doesn't she have an older brother?"

"He's married and moved away."

An oasis of lights appeared against the black backdrop. "Here we are," Noel announced, navigating the vehicle into the yard of a rambling single-story log house with a porch stretched across the front and one side. Cars were parked at odd angles throughout the yard, and Noel wedged his vehicle into a spot alongside the house.

"We'll have to hike up the hill," he informed her with an apologetic grin.

"I wore my boots," she boasted, raising one foot to display her bulky footwear. This time, she'd selected an unfashionable pair with better traction than those she'd worn into town yesterday. Careening around on the ice had created a dangerous situation in more ways than one.

Noel got out and scanned the fleet of cars. "Looks like everybody made it, he assessed. "Chelsea was afraid she'd have to cancel the party if the roads got too bad."

Kate stared up at a clear, star-speckled sky. The night was cold, but beautiful. "I think we've seen the last of the snow for a while. Your friend couldn't have picked a better night for sledding."

Noel extracted a plastic saucer from the back of the vehicle. He carried it by its rope with one hand, reaching for her gloved hand with his other.

Kate thought it was cute. Here was Noel all grown up and protectively holding her hand.

"I've been wanting to talk to you about something that's been bothering me," she said as they followed a path of recent footprints across the snow.

"What?" he asked solemnly.

"Remember the day you locked me out of the house, poured a whole box of laundry detergent into the sink, and left the water running with the stopper on?"

"Yeah. You had to call my dad at the store. Boy, did I ever catch it."

"Whatever possessed you to do such a thing?"

"I was bored and I wanted to see what would happen. Besides, I was mad because I'd seen you in town with Grady. I did have a fierce crush on you."

"That's sweet. Not the part about the soap."

They both laughed.

"Didn't you ever do anything obnoxious when you were a kid?"

She shook her head. "Not really."

The sound of laughter and voices echoing through the night and the bright orange glow of a bonfire drew them toward the hill.

People bundled like mummies in their winter clothing were sliding down the hillside on sleds, tubes, and toboggans, tumbling happily into the snow as they landed.

"Come on, we're missing all the fun," Noel urged,

breaking into a run and pulling her along with him to the foot of the hill.

Suddenly, Katie mischievously released his hand, letting him run on a few feet ahead.

Trailing to a halt, he turned back just in time to see her scoop up a handful of snow.

"This, Noel Dunmore, is your payback for all those bubbles I felt obligated to stay and help clean up," she promised menacingly, aiming her snowball at him.

Noel laughed briefly, holding up his hand defensively. But his expression quickly darkened as his eyes shifted toward the hill.

"Watch out!" a voice called from above, and Katie turned to see a sled barreling down the far end of the hill straight at her.

For an instant, fear paralyzed her, and Noel charged at her. She jumped out of the way at the same moment he valiantly pushed her none too gently, and they both dropped facedown in the snow just in time to feel a sharp breeze as the runaway sled zipped past, missing them by mere inches.

Through snow-caked lashes, she looked over at Noel.

"Are you all right?" she asked after finally catching her breath.

"Just ducky," he said sarcastically. "How about you?"

He sat up and brushed snow off his pant legs.

"You look like a snowman," he observed wryly.

"I'd like to find the idiot who was driving that thing," she complained. "Some people have no regard for . . ."

Snow crunched beneath a flurry of hurried footsteps.

Pressing her palms to the ground, she pushed herself up, squirming in the mass of white powder. She felt like an ant in a sugar bowl.

"Are you hurt?" an all too familiar voice demanded.

She looked up to see Grady bending over her. "We didn't see you when we pushed off."

"What were you doing way over on this side of the hill?" Noel snapped.

Kate was crawling by now. Grady's arms were poised to help her to her feet. A strange warmth rushed through her, color rising to her cheeks as she recalled their encounter in the parking lot yesterday.

She'd come here to forget those disturbing feelings.

"If you hadn't run in front of us . . ." Grady accused Noel.

Kate dodged Grady's outstretched arms and hoisted herself to her feet.

She looked up at him, about to speak, when another face peered over his shoulder.

"Is everybody okay?" the newcomer asked.

Kate recognized her immediately—Grady's friend Libby. The companion, Kate conceded, he seldom traveled without.

Chapter Five

Everyone fell silent.

Grady was watching Kate with anxious eyes. His obvious concern set her stomach grinding. Noel was snarling at Grady as though he'd nearly mowed them down intentionally.

Kate brushed white dust off her sleeve. "It was just a silly little accident," she insisted. "No harm done."

The short woman with the round face and wispy blond hair flashed a relieved smile. Then, as recognition set in, anxiety shadowed her expression.

She glanced briefly up at Grady before swinging her eyes back to Kate. "I *am* sorry," she emphasized, as though she'd committed some unpardonable offense.

Kate raised her chin. Such solicitous behavior was

the last thing she wanted. She knew Grady had told Libby they were old friends. She bristled now, envisioning the two of them having a cozy chat about her. Maybe Shady Pointe had been the wrong place to come to banish her nightmares.

In any event, the atmosphere was far too grim for such a minor incident. When she looked back at Grady, she saw his concern had evaporated. Something else was playing in his eyes, and she realized indignantly he was struggling to keep from laughing. He knew it would take more than a tumble in the snow to do her in.

The tension ebbed out of her, but she couldn't help noticing how Grady poised one gloved hand at the waistline of the woman's parka and leaned close over her shoulder. Kate knew she had no right to resent seeing them so comfortable with each other, but still she did.

She set her hands on her hips. ''Actually,'' she asserted, ''I am a little miffed.''

Libby's eyes widened.

''I was just about to clobber Noel with a snowball,'' Kate lamented.

Grady pulled Libby closer to him. ''Katie and Noel are obviously unscathed,'' he proclaimed with a sly smile. ''I've seen Katie slide into third base harder than that. And Noel, well, boulders would bounce off his head.''

Noel stepped closer beside Katie. "Are you imply-
ing I'm hardheaded?" he asked.

Their initial argument had eased into good-natured
ribbing, and Kate was thankful to Grady for that.

"Settle down," she cajoled.

"It wasn't his fault," Libby added, shooting Grady
a stern look. "Next time, I'm steering.

Kate shook her head. "He never could handle a sled
properly." Then, she grew serious. "I saw you at
Noel's parents' house the other night, but I'm afraid
we haven't officially met." She offered a handshake.
"I'm Kate Smithers."

The petite woman quickly accepted her proffered
hand, shaking it lightly but firmly. "Libby Drew," she
volunteered. "I've heard so much about you. Everyone in town brags about your success. You're practically a local legend. I'm glad to finally know you. And
all my kids are crazy about Calico Crissie."

Kate blinked blankly.

"Libby teaches third grade," Grady explained.

"Oh!" Kate exclaimed. "Well, it's good to know
you, Libby. I'm happy to see Shady Pointe's getting
some younger teachers in the schools." She glanced
up at Grady. "We had to endure the likes of Mrs.
Ziffretti and Mrs. Bean. She wore little polka-dot bows
in her hair every day—a different color for each day
of the week."

Grady laughed lightly. "Monday was red."

Katie turned back to Libby. "She was a sweet

woman, but I'm sure she was well past retirement age when she was teaching us.''

"She finally did retire," Grady reported.

"But not until after I'd graduated," Noel complained.

Grady gave him a droll look. For some reason Kate didn't understand, Grady seemed peeved with Noel. "She lives over in Copper Hollow. She has an old beagle named Jones and I don't know which of the two is keeping the other alive. She's been pretty sick," Grady said seriously.

Kate's voice dropped. "That makes me feel bad about all the dirty tricks we played on her. Moving books around to where she couldn't find them. Someone hid her glasses one day, and then she started wearing them around her neck with a cord.''

"And even then she couldn't find them," Grady recalled with a chuckle. "I suppose I shouldn't have done that.''

Kate gasped. "You, Grady? You never told me that.''

"I've never been especially proud of it. Some of the guys dared me. They figured I was the last person she'd suspect.''

Kate looked up and noticed Noel and Libby were standing off to one side exchanging uncomfortable glances. She realized she and Grady had shut the other two out of the conversation. For a second, she'd almost forgotten their presence.

From Grady's sheepish expression, he seemed to have become aware of the same thing.

He shifted his stance. "I think we can get a few more runs in on the sled before we turn into icebergs," he told Libby.

Libby nodded, then turned back to Kate. "It really was good meeting you. You're such a terrific role model for the kids. I know it's short notice, but they would get such a kick out of having you as a guest at our Christmas party Tuesday afternoon. I don't want to impose, but could you come?"

"I'd be glad to," Kate agreed. Libby's being so nice didn't make things any easier.

Grady shot her a baffled look as he and Libby started back up the hill. "Remember, I'm steering," Libby admonished him in her schoolteacher's warning tone.

Kate was even more surprised to find Noel scowling at her when she turned back.

She couldn't imagine what she'd done to inspire such harsh looks from both him and Grady.

"Is my head on backward?" she asked.

"I don't know. Is it?" he asked. "If you're really over Grady, you don't need to make friends with Libby to prove it."

"I like Libby," she defended herself. "Who wouldn't? She asked me for a favor, and I'm going to do it for the kids, show them there's more available to them and their futures than what they see here every day. This has nothing to do with Grady. He and I broke up a long time ago.''

''I know that. The question is, are you wishing now things had worked out differently?''

''Honestly, Noel. Grady and I scarcely know each other anymore. We're just a little uncomfortable with each other because of some lingering hurt feelings on both sides.''

''For a few minutes there, the two of you didn't seem at all uncomfortable with each other.''

Kate's skin reddened. ''We got caught up in old school memories. Maybe you'll understand when you get a few years older.''

''Mom believes Grady never married because he never got over you.''

Her brow narrowed. ''And vice versa?''

''Natch.''

''Until I ran into Grady at your parents' house the other night, I hadn't given him a thought in years,'' she lied, hating herself for it. ''And obviously, he's gone on with his life, despite your mom's theory. Libby seems perfect for him.''

''You don't have to get so defensive. You know how Mom is with her romantic ideas about undying love and all that.''

''Well, that stuff makes for good movies, but life doesn't always play out that way. Now, I believe there's a snowball around here somewhere with your name on it.''

Noel obligingly let her pelt him with a few snow-balls, although the snow was so powdery, they practically disintegrated in midair.

He challenged her to a race up the hill and beat her mercilessly.

At the top of the hill, she was introduced to their hostess, Chelsea, a dark-haired, soft-spoken, earthy young woman with merriment sparkling in her green eyes. Most of the other guests were teachers and people Kate had met the other night at Noel's house. Many, like Noel, had returned to Shady Pointe to visit their families for the holidays.

Kate and Noel tried all the snow toys the Bartletts had assembled for their guests—sleds, toboggans, and saucers. Between runs Kate warmed herself by the raging fire and sipped hot cocoa or mulled cider poured from insulated jugs.

She was determined to have as good a time as anyone else here, and Noel's endless energy left her little opportunity to dwell on her problems or to pick Grady and Libby out in the crowd.

Still, shutting Grady out completely was difficult. She kept thinking she heard his voice above the others. Over the past years, she had sometimes thought of Grady and missed the warm relationship they'd shared. This evening was the first time the thought had occurred to her that maybe she'd made a horrible mistake when she'd chosen a dream in New York over a future here with him.

"Come on," Noel coaxed, brushing a handful of yellow hair out of his eyes. The wind had picked up, driving many of the sledders into the farmhouse below. Shivering, Kate had to admit the bright lights and smoke spiraling out of the chimney sure looked appealing. "Let's take one last ride down the hill."

"Okay," she agreed. "But it's my turn to steer."

He stepped aside so she could mount first, then boarded behind her, cinching his arms around her waist.

"Ready?" she asked.

"Go!" he called back, pushing off with one foot.

Kate laughed as the sled picked up speed, her hat flying off and the wind whipping her hair into Noel's face.

He whooped like a rodeo bronc rider.

Her hair streamed back, and Kate opened herself to the exhilaration of skimming through the snow. For a few seconds, she was a girl again. How many thousands of times had she done this? She felt so suddenly and wonderfully alive, it almost hurt.

"Yee-ha!" Noel hollered again, his antics raising her laughter to a higher tempo. At the bottom of the hill, she guided the slowing sled to a stop. She was laughing so hard her stomach hurt.

"I feel like I'm five years old again," Kate sputtered when she was finally able to speak. She got off the sled.

Noel startled her by blanketing her in a quick, warm

hug. "Good," he asserted finally as he took her hand and began leading her toward the farmhouse. "You've got a nice laugh, you know. Sounds like bells ringing."

"Oh, come on, Noel—bells ringing?"

"I mean it."

As Kate took a last glance up the hill, she saw Grady suddenly turn and walk away from the spot where he'd been poised on the hilltop, watching.

Flurries began fluttering from the night sky before they reached the farmhouse, and Kate heard a collective groan rise up among those remaining on the hill. She was so numb from cold she could barely feel her toes.

She was ready for the warm atmosphere the Bartletts' home provided. A fire blazed in the stone fireplace on one end of a spacious living room decorated cheerfully in pine and plaids. The paneling and exposed beams overhead enhanced the interior's rustic look.

The walls were draped with evergreen garlands and huge red velvet bows; vanilla-scented candles burned atop the hearth. A popular song was playing on the stereo. Guests were scattered throughout the room—talking, dancing, sipping hot mulled cider, and munching miniature sandwiches, chips, dips, and other assorted finger foods from a generously laden buffet table.

Although everyone was winding down from the activity on the hill and warming themselves, the party didn't seem to have lost any velocity. Inside the heated room, Kate realized how thoroughly chilled she was.

"I'll get you some cider, and we can sit by the fire," Noel offered. "Do you want something to eat?"

She shook her head. "Not just yet, thanks."

"I'll be right back," he promised.

She found a place for them by the fire. As she watched Noel wind through the crowd, she wondered if he wouldn't be happier mingling among his friends instead of being burdened with her.

Once she sat down, she swept her gaze across the room. Grady and Libby were slow-dancing, talking intently as they moved to the music. They must have come in right behind her and Noel.

Unwarranted jealousy speared her. Quickly, feeling like an intruder, she averted her gaze. She shouldn't begrudge Grady or anyone else their happiness. Even under the improbable possibility that she was still in love with him, she should be wishing him the best. Shouldn't she be glad he'd found Libby? She herself had nothing to offer him or anyone else. Ultimately, she had to resign herself to seeing them together.

"There you are," Noel said, approaching with a Styrofoam cup balanced in each hand. She accepted the one he handed her, sniffing the contents and enjoying the spicy aroma of the hot cider.

"Thanks," she told him.

"My pleasure."

"Not just for the cider. For tonight. I've had more fun than I've had in a long time. But don't feel obligated to sit here with me. If you want to go off and talk to your friends, it's all right."

He planted himself beside her. "You refuse to understand, don't you? This is exactly where I want to be. You're not starting to feel like you're baby-sitting again, are you?"

She chuckled. "You're slightly better behaved these days."

He shook his head. "You were a saint. My parents couldn't possibly have paid you enough to put up with me."

"They didn't."

"Why did you subject yourself to my shenanigans, then?"

"I knew it wasn't easy being an only child. Besides, it was kind of interesting, waiting to see what you were going to come up with next."

He rolled his eyes. "In other words, you pitied my lonely existence."

"Noel?" a new voice broke into their conversation.

Kate followed his glance as he looked up and found Chelsea standing over him, her hands clasped behind her back.

"Say, Chelsea," he greeted her. "Great party."

"It really is," Kate echoed.

The young woman smiled brightly. Her glance

dropped back to Noel, and her dark brow knit. "I'm trying to find someone who can do a Texas two-step."

Noel slapped his forehead and groaned. "Chelsea's into country music," he explained to Kate.

Chelsea nodded enthusiastically. "I want to put some on, but I'm afraid nobody will get out there and try to dance to it. Anyway, Samantha Dowling says you can two-step. I thought if we went out there first . . ."

"And Samantha swore she'd never tell."

"Come on, Noel."

Kate could tell by the younger woman's expression she wasn't searching for just any dance partner. Noel didn't seem to notice, but she obviously adored him. Once again, Kate felt guilty for monopolizing his attention. She was using him like a shield, she realized, and it wasn't fair.

"Go on," she urged him.

"Are you sure, Kate?" he asked.

"Really. I want to see this."

"Thanks, Ms. Smithers," Chelsea said, snagging Noel's arm. As the two of them headed for the area cleared for dancing, Kate felt about a thousand and five years old.

Still, she took pride in sending them off together, thinking of someone else finally. She'd been feeling calm and content, but now restlessness rolled through her like a tidal wave. She'd felt better than she had any right to. Only by some quirky cosmic choice was she here, and she shouldn't forget. . . .

She shifted uneasily. The room, the crowd, the music seemed to be closing in on her.

Desperately needing fresh air, she got up and crossed the room to the bedroom where the coats were piled atop a double bed. She dug through them to find hers. Stuffing her arms into it, she stepped back out to the party and slipped unnoticed out the side door.

Standing on the porch, she folded her arms against the wind and gazed out across the moonlit snowscape. The earlier flurries had dissipated instead of spinning into a full-fledged snowstorm, but the wind remained sharp. Dark clouds formed a black latticework across the night sky. No stars were visible, and she could scarcely see the moon.

Suddenly, a falling star blazed a fiery path through the darkness, vanishing as quickly as a camera flash.

Kate stiffened as though she had been shot.

How bizarre life was that details infinitesimal in the grand scale of things could change it forever. In one split second, one heartbeat, a star had disappeared from the universe. But such a breathtaking exit.

She felt so hatefully selfish. Tonight, for a while, she'd allowed herself to feel glad to be alive.

"Katie?"

She recognized Grady's voice before she turned to face him. There was no place to escape to.

"You shouldn't have followed me out here,

Grady,'' she told him. His deep brown eyes were focused so intently on her, she felt shivery inside.

''I saw you leave. You looked so lost all of a sudden . . .''

She traced the wooden railing with her fingers. ''You know, I should have been the one who was killed in that plane crash.''

''You can't mean that.''

''The man who was killed, Harold Young, was a good friend. He worked as my assistant, practically helped me build the company.'' She took a deep breath, then continued. ''He was thirty-five years old, and he was anxious to get home that night because it was his daughter's birthday. He and his wife had two children. I could have gone to that meeting in New Orleans without him, but he was so good, so quick with facts and figures . . .''

Grady moved closer but did not touch her. ''Stop browbeating yourself. You couldn't have known. It was his time, not yours.''

''He had so much to live for.''

''And you don't? Honey, you've kept hope alive in this town for years now. You've accomplished more than you know.''

She shrugged, biting back tears.

''Is it worth so much?''

''I know I let you down, but . . .''

Her head snapped up. ''You let me down?''

''Don't you remember the plan? As soon as you

finished college and I finished vet school we were both going to move away. I was the one who backed out and decided to stay here.''

"Because your brother could have been dying. I knew you had to stay, and yet I couldn't.''

"I knew you couldn't. How do you think I would have felt if you'd given up your future because of me? That's why I never tried to convince you to stay.''

She swallowed hard. "I thought it was because . . .''

"Because I didn't care enough? No, Katie, I never stopped caring. I thought I had, but when I saw you walk into the Dunmores' living room the other night . . .''

Shaking her head, she stepped back.

"Don't say it. Please. I know you're trying to make me feel better, but this isn't helping.''

"I'm not asking you to pick up where we left off, Katie. But there's a part of me that's always going to care about you. It's frightening to hear you say your life's not worth anything.''

"Please go back inside. Just let go, Grady. You must be freezing, and I'm sure Libby is wondering where you are.''

"Libby knows where I am.''

Of course she did. It wasn't like Grady to sneak away from a date to talk to his former fiancée. Hiding old Mrs. Bean's glasses was probably the most dishonest thing he'd ever done.

"I came out here because I thought you might need

a shoulder to cry on. But as usual, you don't. I suggest you go back inside before you throw poor Noel into a panic. But we are definitely not finished with this discussion, Katie. There are too many loose ends you and I need to resolve.''

It seemed to her he had resolved them already.

Chapter Six

Saturday morning, after Kate's parents left for a
shopping trip to the mall in Penworthy, she poured
herself a second cup of coffee and settled down in the
living room with a box of dolls from her old collection
she'd rummaged out of the attic.

Outside, the sky was overcast and gloomy. She was
starting to wonder if the sun was ever going to shine
again.

Dressed in jeans and an old sweater, she sat cross-
legged on the floor, digging out her precious dolls one
by one, as surprised and delighted as a child on Christmas morning as she inspected her long-forgotten treasures.

The radio hummed softly in the background; logs

crackled in the fireplace. She'd plugged in the Christmas tree lights, creating her own cozy little haven. She refused to give in to the gray mood the weather inspired.

The dolls were in pretty good shape despite having been stored so long. Her mother had carefully wrapped each one in paper and plastic to keep out moisture. Kate reflected guiltily she'd left them on a shelf in her room. She'd felt such a compelling need to leave Shady Pointe. As though her life wouldn't go on until she did.

Now, as she unwrapped the dolls, she began lining them against the sofa—the porcelain bride doll, the plastic Kewpie, the soft Raggedy Ann. She'd begun collecting them as a young teen, at the same time most girls were putting theirs away. But she'd been studying hers, not playing with them. She'd noted the tiny details, how they were made.

The shrill ring of the phone interrupted her reverie. She was tempted to ignore it, but her parents could be having car trouble and needing help. She set down the baby doll that drank and wet, then got up.

''Hello?'' she answered.

''Kate. How are you?'' At once, Kate recognized her general manager's lilting voice.

''Fine, Madison, is anything wrong?''

''Nothing. Don't worry—really, I've got everything under control.''

''Great.''

"So when are you coming back?"

Kate laughed. "Don't be so subtle. I'm sorry. I've heaped too much responsibility on you, haven't I?"

"No, that's not it. You know I can handle it, even without you and Harold. I just think you should know Pierce Blane was in the office yesterday, snooping around, asking a lot of questions about when you'd be back."

A shiver shot down Kate's spine. "What did you tell him?"

"I told him we were expecting you after the holidays. I asked him if he wanted me to deliver a message or did he need the number where he could contact you. He said no."

Kate felt cold inside. Pierce Blane had invested in her ideas when everyone else thought she was a wild-eyed kid. Without the insightful multimillionaire, she'd have no company, no Calico Crissie. But for the past two years, their ideas had been clashing, and he'd been shamelessly trying to buy her out.

"He's up to something. I wish I knew what."

"He's got a new doll he wants to put into production."

"Gingham Lil—it's the one we've been planning."

"No, it's not yours, Kate. He's found a new designer. I can hold him off for a while, but without you, he's going to take over and ramrod it through."

Kate raked splayed fingers through her hair. She knew what Madison was telling her. If she didn't get back soon, she'd lose control of her own company. But she couldn't leave just yet. Her parents were so excited about having her home for Christmas, and she didn't know that she had the stamina for a showdown with Pierce.

''If he comes back again, tell him I'll be back the day after Christmas and he can either wait and discuss any production changes with me then or call me here.''

''All right.''

''And I appreciate your letting me know, Madison. And everything else you've done. You're a lifesaver.''

Kate hung up, shaking her head. No one should be as rich and powerful, or as bullheaded, as Pierce Blane.

She returned to the living room, but her coffee was cold and her peaceful mood destroyed. She knew she should be on the next plane back to New York. Pierce had a bad habit of walking all over people, and he owned enough of her company to bully her employees into letting him take over.

Not so long ago, her company had been her life. Now, she contemplated the idea of selling out to Blane. The prospect of returning to work failed to generate any of the excitement it once would have. Instead it left her feeling hollow inside.

But if she didn't go back to New York, what would she do? She was far too young to retire. She couldn't stay here where she'd be forced to watch Grady and Libby get married and raise a family.

Suddenly, it struck her why she couldn't bear to witness their happiness. Not by chance did that disturbing tingly feeling come over her whenever he was within twenty feet. And her wanting so much for him to kiss her in the parking lot the other day was no accident either. She was as much in love with him now as she had been when he was seventeen and all arms and legs and lopsided grin.

Okay, so she'd finally acknowledged her feelings to herself. She would never reveal them to Grady. She loved and respected him enough to stay out of his life this time. Avoiding him was the best thing she could do for both of them. She had to go back to New York. Giving up her company would mean accepting defeat, letting life beat her down, and she would not surrender.

Maybe someday, she'd meet someone like Grady. But then, hadn't she been looking unsuccessfully for a long time now?

So why hadn't Madison's phone call spurred her into action? Didn't she care about the business that had once meant everything to her?

She was so absorbed in her thoughts, it took her a moment to realize the doorbell was ringing.

Thinking it must be a salesman, she got up. She was surprised when she looked through the peephole to see Leeann Meredith, Grady's mom, standing on the porch.

Quickly, she pulled open the door.

"Mrs. Meredith!" she greeted her. "I'm afraid my mom's not here right now."

Mrs. Meredith, her arms folded over her red wool jacket, wavy, medium-length brown hair blowing in the wind, shook her head.

"You're the one I've come to see, Kate," she insisted. "Are you busy?"

"No, come in, please," Kate offered, ashamed at her lapse of manners. She'd just been so astounded to see Mrs. Meredith here.

The tall, slender woman rubbed her hands together as she came inside. She seemed to take in everything at once. "Oh, it's nice and warm in here. Miserable outside, isn't it? You've got a fire going. What a lovely doll."

Kate glanced down to see she still carried a nurse doll tucked under one arm.

She shrugged. "I was just going through some of my old stuff from the attic. Can I get you some coffee?"

Mrs. Meredith shook her head briskly. "No, I can't stay. I'm in kind of a jam, and I was wondering if you could help me out, since my family's abandoned me."

"Sure," Kate replied, thinking maybe she needed her battery jumped or a ride somewhere. From what

Kate remembered, she was always juggling about ten activities at one time.

Grady's mom flashed a grateful smile, tossing her hands in the air. "I always get carried away this time of year. The community center is having its children's Christmas party this evening, and I promised to provide cookies. I've got to deliver them by four, and I could use some help. Would you mind terribly?"

"No. I . . . I'd be glad to help you out. Let me close the fireplace doors and get my coat."

"Used to be I had too many helpers when I baked. Now everybody's busy, with their families and friends and jobs. Grady's got the clinic open on Saturday mornings, not that he'd ever bake a cookie. He sure enjoys eating them though."

Kate realized this was Mrs. Meredith's way of letting her know her son wasn't likely to pop into the kitchen this morning.

Mrs. Meredith paused. "I suppose I could cheat and pick up something at the supermarket, but I think the kids deserve something special, homemade, you know? I hope I'm not imposing . . ."

"No, Mrs. Meredith. I'd be happy to help, really."

"Terrific. But, please, call me Leeann."

Kate had always felt a little uncomfortable around Grady's mom. She was organized, efficient, and had set ideas about the way things should be done. And she'd never been shy about speaking her mind. Kate never knew how Mrs. Meredith felt about her breakup with Grady so long ago, but she had an inkling she was going to find out.

Surprisingly, as Kate relaxed, she began to enjoy the baking session. Leeann had an extensive collection of recipes she'd obtained from friends and family members and a knack for telling hilarious anecdotes. "It's always so hard trying to decide which ones to make," she reflected, looking over Kate's shoulder as the younger woman scanned her recipe file.

Soon, the spacious yellow-and-white kitchen smelled of cinnamon, ginger, and nutmeg. Kate found a fundamental peace in rolling and cutting dough. After the first batches were done, Leeann implemented Kate's artistic talents, setting her to work decorating cookies with red, green, and white icing and an assortment of sprinkles and candies. She asked endless questions about life in New York, but mentioned neither the accident nor Grady.

With several dozen decorated cookies completed, Leeann fixed them each a cup of tea, and sat at the cluttered table catty-corner from Kate.

Looking thoughtful, she dipped the tea bag in her cup.

Here it comes, Kate thought. *She's going to give me what-for.*

"I was glad to hear you've been getting out more," the older woman said finally. "I've found staying busy takes your mind off your problems."

"I've always been amazed at how you manage to get so much done."

"I'm just used to it. Kate, I know your accident was really a big shock to you, but everything happens for a reason. People waste a lot of time looking for answers they aren't going to find. The brighter side of this tragedy is it brought you back to Shady Pointe at a time when you're needed most."

Kate looked incredulous. "Why could you possibly think I'm needed here?"

"I'm sure you've heard this town's falling to pieces. Mike has had to travel farther and farther away from home on his construction jobs for the past two years, sometimes staying out of town for days at a time. The kids are growing up, moving away, and we never envisioned spending so much time apart. We're putting the house up for sale after the first of the year."

"Does Grady know?" The words spilled out of her mouth before she could stop them.

"No. We're not telling any of our children until we finally make a decision."

Kate contemplated a copper bowl full of ivy suspended by chains from the ceiling. "If Grady knew, it might convince him to run for mayor. A lot of people have been urging him to run."

Leeann nixed that idea. "Grady doesn't want to be mayor. Can you see him, taking the oath of office in that awful plaid fishing hat he always used to wear?" She laughed brightly.

Remembering the gaudy hat Grady had never seemed to be without for several of his younger years, Kate smiled appreciatively. "He was really upset when he lost that hat."

"Which is why I never told him I hid it. And don't you tell him either."

"I wouldn't. I doubt if I'll be seeing him again."

"Of course you will. People here are looking to Grady as the answer to all their problems. He heals their sick animals, so they think he can accomplish anything. That's the problem with these folks—they've sat back for so long letting Hewett run everything, they want to keep sitting back and let someone else fix it all now. It's not that simple. And I think people are being too hasty in pointing the finger at Hewett."

"So what are you trying to say?"

"Shady Pointe is your home. You're creative, resourceful, and you know how to strike a bargain. Surely you have some ideas on how we can pump life into this town. I have dear, old friends here. I've watched their children grow up along with my own. I don't want to leave. Have you considered what it might mean to this town if you stayed?"

Kate knew she couldn't stay here. "I'm needed back in New York. I did have an idea I thought might work here," Kate admitted. "But Grady was pretty discouraging when I brought it up."

Leeann raised one eyebrow. "And you're letting that stop you?"

Kate glanced down at the table top. "It was a pretty impulsive suggestion. And Grady was probably right. I was wondering," she said slowly, "about Grady and Libby."

"You mean how serious are they?" Leeann asked, fending the question in stride. "It took you long enough to get around to asking. They've been seeing each other for a couple of years now. As far as I know, neither one dates anyone else, but there's no formal engagement. Now, would you like some more tea?"

When Kate didn't answer immediately, Leeann paused to raise an eyebrow. "I'm fond of Libby, Kate. And I'm sure Grady is too, but he's never discussed his feelings about her with me. After you left, he didn't date anyone steadily for a long time. He wouldn't admit it, but I think I he had a hard time getting over you. Then he met Libby. I do know he's upset that she's considering leaving Shady Pointe."

Kate's eyes shot up to meet Leeann's warm brown ones. How far would Grady go to keep Libby from moving away?

"He must care for Libby very much," Kate observed.

Leeann shrugged. "Perhaps he's weighing how much." Her voice softened. "For what it's worth, Kate, I know no one ever gets what she wants out of life by stepping aside."

Kate busied herself rearranging cookies on the platter. She knew Mrs. Meredith meant well, but she couldn't latch on to Grady like a lifeboat. In her present state, she had nothing to offer anyone. Maybe someday, if she ever started to feel normal again . . .

"I was just curious," she countered quickly, though her tongue felt thick. "Libby seems perfect for Grady."

Leeann flashed her a quizzical look but said only, "Let's get those gingerbread men out of the oven. They'll be loads of fun to decorate."

At four-fifteen that afternoon, Kate found herself helping Mrs. Meredith deliver cookies to the Shady Pointe Community Center, an aging, drafty building that had been sorely in need of repairs for years. The city could never seem to find the money.

Still, Leeann and her friends, mostly volunteers from local churches, had stubbornly made the old place festive with garlands and twinkling lights and red and white poinsettias. A fat pine tree, so tall its tip nearly touched the ceiling, was decorated at the front of the hall. Its branches dripped tinsel. Each place setting at the long tables boasted a red or green toy train car brimming with candies.

The room was buzzing with children and parents and scurrying volunteers.

"Where did all these kids come from?" Kate asked over her shoulder after she and Leeann had deposited the last load of cookies in the kitchen. When no answer came, she whipped around to discover Mrs. Meredith had drifted off into the crowd.

Kate feared the older woman's friends had gotten hold of her and roped her into another chore. If so, Kate would be stuck here for hours. The center was a few blocks off the downtown area, close enough to walk home in mild weather, but too far to walk today. Since her departure this morning was unplanned, she had worn only tennis shoes instead of boots.

Not seeing Leeann nearby, Kate went through the double doors to the back of the hall. Passing the kitchen, she glanced inside but didn't see her neighbor among the workers. Where could she have vanished to?

The sound of crying drew her farther back into the building. It was dark, and the narrow halls turned and twisted like a maze. But the sound grew louder, and at last, near the back door, she discovered a tiny girl with round green eyes and curly blond hair that fell across her shoulders. The child, who couldn't have been more than four, looked up at her as she approached. She was wearing white tights and a faded but pressed lacy red party dress.

The girl obviously needed help, but Kate considered how to approach her without startling her. She knew in today's world most children were by necessity taught not to speak to strangers.

"I'll bet you're lost," Kate said finally.

The girl nodded.

''The party's back up front. Your mom's probably up there. Do you want me to take you to her?''

She extended her hand, but the little girl shied away.

Good girl, Kate thought. She'd been taught well. But how could she get the girl back to her mother?

Considering her problem, she looked up in time to see Santa ambling up the hall. His thin frame was out of proportion to the mound of padding over his belly, and his walk was awfully familiar. A brown-haired boy about ten or eleven walked by his side.

Kate watched as they approached, doing a double take when Santa winked at her. His brown eyes sparkled above the cottony white fake beard.

It was Grady, she realized, unable to help smiling at him. Who could resist smiling at Santa Claus? And Grady looked uncomfortable enough in the suit to appear almost comical.

Except she knew how serious his intentions were to have consented to this.

''Here she is,'' he told the boy, who immediately took the girl by the arm. ''Mom's been looking all over for you, Becky. You are in for it.''

Grady leaned over the girl, whose face lit up in fascination. She ignored her brother and raised a chubby hand to pat Grady's beard.

''Santa,'' she said.

''You need to go back to your mom, Becky,'' he advised. ''Or you'll miss getting your present.''

As her older brother led her back toward the front, he called, "Thanks, Dr. Meredith—I mean, Santa."

Turning to Kate, he rolled his eyes. "So much for maintaining the mystery. What are you doing here?"

Kate pulled her coat lapels together, suddenly conscious of her disheveled appearance—the faded, flour-streaked jeans, the shapeless gray sweater, her hair pulled back haphazardly, her face lacking makeup.

"Your mom recruited me into baking."

He nodded understandingly. "Watch out for Mom. She's always soliciting volunteers. She had me on the roof, stringing Christmas lights this year."

He reached out so unexpectedly, Kate didn't have a chance to dodge the fingertip that touched her cheek. She could have sworn sparks were flying as he made a quick sweeping motion.

"Buttercream icing?" he asked.

"Oh, gosh," she muttered, raising a hand to her chin. "Is there any more?"

He laughed. "No."

"I must look like a hobo."

He stopped laughing. "You look great. You always do. In fact, you look more today like I remember you—relaxed, happy."

Kate stiffened. She had no right to be happy.

He gave her a hard look and seemed to be on the verge of saying more.

"I've got to get in to the kids," was all he said. "My fans are waiting."

Kate watched him go, her heart swelling. Anyone else who hated wearing that costume as much as she knew Grady must would have refused to wear it. But he loved this town and he loved kids as well as animals.

Curious, she migrated back to the party, where Grady was just about to make his entrance.

She leaned against the wall, watching as kids walked up one by one to get their gifts. After they talked to Santa, one of the elves behind them would hand the child a wrapped present.

At her post to the side, Kate was one of few people who noticed Grady slip a hand in his pocket and press a bill into one little boy's hand.

"That's Joshua Donaldson. His mom's in the hospital, and his dad's out of work," a voice whispered over her shoulder. Kate glanced sideways and saw Mrs. Meredith had materialized.

Kate leaned toward her. "Will she be okay? His mom?"

Leeann's expression furrowed. "We're all hoping, but I understand it's quite serious."

Kate hadn't been paying much attention to the elves, until one, at a break between children, waved at them. She realized it was Libby. Now Kate understood. Donning the Santa suit hadn't been Grady's idea. A familiar sense of detachment flooded through her.

"I'm ready to go if you're through here," Kate announced.

"All right," Leeann agreed.

She chatted amicably on the way home but mercifully didn't mention Grady or Libby again.

"Thanks so much for your help," she said as she dropped Kate off at her parents' house. "I enjoyed spending the afternoon with you."

Kate saw not only had her parents returned, but there was an unfamiliar car in the driveway, a late-model maroon sedan.

She hoped she could slip upstairs inconspicuously. If her parents had company, she didn't want to disturb them, and she was in no mood for entertaining.

To that end, she decided to use the side door, but no sooner was she on the landing than her mom was calling out to her. "Kate?"

Kate had no choice but to make an appearance. She didn't want to be rude to her parents' friends.

A fresh fire was blazing in the fireplace, and the tree lights were on. A gray-haired couple sat perched on the sofa, facing the Smitherses. A tray of cheese sticks and sliced apples centered the coffee table, and soft-drink glasses sat on coasters on the end tables.

Ordinarily, Kate would have found nothing unusual or troubling about her parents entertaining on a Saturday night. It was who these people were that bothered her.

She froze in the doorway.

"Kate," her mother prodded. "You remember our friends, Mr. and Mrs. Sparks, don't you?"

Stunned, Kate nodded feebly. "How are you, Mayor? Mrs. Sparks?"

Chapter Seven

"You're just the person I was hoping to see," Hewett Sparks told her after a round of polite greetings.

"Me?" Kate asked. "Why, Mr. Sparks?"

Sparks was a big man. The couch seemed to shrink beneath his long, broad frame. His head dropped, then he looked up again.

"I guess you've noticed this town has changed while you've been gone."

Fallen apart, you mean, she thought, but she merely gave a polite nod.

"You've probably heard folks blaming me for all the problems."

She opened her mouth to speak, then thought better of it. Her parents had raised her to respect her elders.

To her amazement, Hewett laughed, swiping a beefy hand through the air. "Don't be shy about hurting my feelings. When you've been mayor as long as I have, you let most of the rumblings bounce off. People always have something to gripe about. I doubt you've heard anything worse than I already have."

Kate pursed her lips. "What goes on here is really none of my concern," she suggested tactfully. "After all, I don't live in Shady Pointe anymore."

"Which is exactly why I'd like to hear your views on what Shady Pointe needs. Everyone who lives here is looking out for his own interests first. You know this town, you know how to get things done, but you're in a position to be objective."

Kate tried to determine whether he really wanted to hear what she had to say or whether he was asking only to win her, and especially her parents, over to his side.

Her first thought was to say Shady Pointe needed to offer more opportunity, a chance for everyone to make a good living and things to do to make living here more enjoyable. But why point out the obvious?

Something more important needed to take place before anything improved.

"All the cliques and the bickering are killing this town. Nothing will get any better until all of you pull together and come up with a plan."

He shook his head thoughtfully. "That, young lady, is easier said than done."

Kate began to suspect he was fishing for information, maybe wondering what she'd heard the younger people in town saying, maybe wondering whether Grady really planned to run against him.

"If I were you, I'd start by convincing people I wasn't doing special favors for my friends. Word is a zoning ordinance was enforced to close down Mable Osgood's shop to spare Mrs. Trent the competition."

Evie Sparks' mouth flew open indignantly. "Has Mabel been saying that?"

Her husband calmed her with a hand on her arm.

Kate shook her head. "No. I haven't even seen Mrs. Osgood since I've been back. Getting emotional about issues doesn't help. I'm just telling you how people feel."

Hewett leaned forward, propping his elbows on his knees. He leveled his dark eyes on her. "The truth is, Kate, Mabel's neighbors complained about the traffic congestion and parking. That area is zoned residential. The zoning board wouldn't change it, because Mabel doesn't have a big enough driveway for her customers to park in."

"She has a huge yard. Would the board reconsider if she put in a small parking lot?"

"Of course. As long as her neighbors don't object, there's no problem. No one wants to keep her from earning some money."

"What about Vine's building?"

He shrugged. "That's beyond my control."

"Well, what if the city rented it until it's sold? Local people could rent spaces to sell their crafts or paintings or produce."

"There's an idea. But you have to understand, everything has to go through the city council. If you think people in this town are squabbling, you should come to one of the council meetings."

Kate was almost enjoying bouncing ideas around. So many times she and Harold and a consultant or an artist had locked themselves in the conference room and tossed out the most outlandish ideas until they found one they could use. She felt best when her brain was working, she realized. But she'd also been long overdue for a break in the demands she made on herself. Maybe that boardroom was where she belonged. It would never be the same without Harold helping her. She would always miss her good friend, but she had to go on. She couldn't really live if she stopped letting herself generate ideas.

"I shouldn't be telling you your business," she said.

"I asked, didn't I?" Sparks insisted. "But I'm afraid it's going to take more than I can do to bring this town together."

Kate raised an eyebrow. "You're not running for reelection then?"

"No."

"Will you be supporting another candidate?"

He locked his hands together. "I always thought my son Dan would run when I gave it up. I've always wanted the best for Shady Pointe. But everything's gotten out of control. Anyway, Dan's youngest son started college in the fall, and he and his wife have decided to move to California. I'm tired of catching the blame for everything that goes wrong. Let someone else take a shot at it. I was trying to talk your dad into running."

"And I said no," her dad added quickly.

Kate smiled softly, masking her relief. She could understand why no one would want the headaches of trying to unite a divided town.

"Maybe you should call a town meeting. Make people understand everyone needs to pitch in."

His face brightened. "Would you come? If they heard some of these ideas of yours . . ."

Kate shook her head. "It's not my place. Besides, I'll be leaving after the holidays."

"It's a shame. People around here look up to you."

"I'm sorry. But I'm sure you'll find a way to turn things around." She folded her arms. She'd had a long day, and she needed some air and time alone. She turned to her mom. "I think I'm going to walk up to Baker's and get a hamburger."

"There's deli ham and coleslaw in the refrigerator," Julia Smithers protested.

Kate shook her head. "Thanks, but I've got a craving for a burger. I haven't had one of Baker's since I've been home.''

''Be careful,'' Julia called.

''Nice to have you on our side,'' Hewett Sparks called out. Kate shuddered inwardly. Hadn't he been listening? She wasn't taking sides. She wondered if he'd been sincere about wanting change, if he was truly being unfairly held responsible for the town's problems. Just because he said he wouldn't run for reelection didn't mean he wouldn't change his mind later. What if nobody ran?

Well, she certainly couldn't work any magic here. In coming back to her hometown, she'd hoped people would treat her like plain old Kate Smithers. Then maybe she'd start feeling normal again.

She shot out the side door. Although it was dark out, she felt safe in Shady Pointe. Besides, she'd taken a self-defense class in New York and knew how to look out for herself.

Baker's, a combination lunch counter and grocery store, was only a few blocks away. Halfway there, Kate realized she'd left the house once again in thin tennis shoes and hadn't covered her head. *Dumb,* she thought, quickening her pace.

As she rounded the corner, reassured to see the familiar lights of the little family-owned shop, a vehicle slowed down beside her.

Alarmed, she snapped her glance sideways, surprised to see Grady edge his Explorer to the curb. Ollie was in the back, craning his bandanna-clad neck over the seat. Grady was watching something down the sidewalk.

"Get in," he ordered in a low, calm voice.

Halting, Kate set her hands on her hips. "Why?" she demanded, seeing no reason for her to comply nor for him to speak to her so roughly. But deep inside fear stabbed her. Something had to be terribly wrong for Grady to act this way.

Grady flashed her an angry, exasperated look, then got out of the Explorer and stepped onto the sidewalk. He didn't speak until he was nearly nose-to-nose with her.

His voice was harsh but barely above a whisper. "You're being followed," he informed her.

When she gasped, he flashed her a warning look. "Just get in the car like you're glad I happened by."

She held her breath as she marched to the vehicle. Once in, she couldn't resist looking down the street.

"I don't see anyone," she reported.

"I didn't see him the other day when you did, so that makes us even," Grady told her as he buckled his seat belt.

Kate swallowed hard. "Are you sure it wasn't just someone who happened to be out walking?"

"Yes. He came out of a van parked near my parents' house after you started down the street. I was on my way to drop the Santa suit off to Mom, and followed him to see what he was up to. I'm sure he was trailing you. Buckle up.''

Her hands knotted into fists. ''A reporter. I'm sure of it. If he's found me, others will. I'm going to have to leave Shady Pointe before Christmas. At least in New York, I can deal with the press without having my friends' and family's privacy invaded.''

He leaned across her and fastened her seat belt. ''You don't need to spend Christmas away from your home. And you don't need to talk to reporters if you don't want to.''

''Grady, I've dealt with the press before. A legitimate journalist would have approached me and asked for an interview by now. This guy is after a different kind of story. Watching me, taking notes, maybe talking to people behind my back. In any case, how I'm coping after my accident is no one's business but my own.''

Grady was grinning.

''I don't see any humor in this.''

''Listen to yourself. It's nice to hear you get mad. Reminds me of someone I used to know, a girl who'd take on an army if someone's rights were being trampled.''

Startled, Katie blinked. He was right, though—she was furious. ''This is serious, Grady. He's probably been snapping pictures of me everywhere I go. If he knows where I am . . .''

''For the moment he knows. I've got a cabin at

Echo Lake, and I do mean a cabin. But there's heat and electricity, and solitude if you can stand it."

"You'd let me stay there? But I'm sure he knows my car."

"You'll take the Explorer. I can borrow my brother's old junker . . ."

"Grady! I can't let you do that."

"Katie, do you honestly want to go back to New York right now?"

"No."

"So let me do this. I know your parents are looking forward to having you here for Christmas."

So, he was doing this for their sake, not hers. "All right. But we'll trade vehicles so you won't have to borrow your brother's."

"Okay. Done. Let's go back and get your things."

"Grady?"

"Hmm?"

"Thanks."

"Don't mention it. The cabin's just sitting there empty anyway."

For several minutes, they rode in heavy, reflective silence until Grady broke it.

"Maybe it's none of my business, Katie, but Hall Dunwood doesn't strike me as your type."

For a reason she couldn't explain, she felt relieved at his being curious enough to finally ask.

"He was dating a friend of mine who was convinced our ad agency should hire him to do our commercials. I knew his image didn't mesh with our product, but for her sake I agreed to have dinner with the two of them so I could meet him. Stephanie arrived late intentionally, sure I'd be dazzled by him. During those strained few minutes while we waited for her a photographer, who'd been following him, snapped our picture. To make matters worse, Hall was furious. He made a scene and had the guy ejected from the restaurant, which sparked more interest in the whole episode. My small notoriety as the creator of Calico Crissie got blown out of proportion. I've never been so embarrassed as I was when those papers printed that picture and insinuated Hall and I were having some secret romance. I ignored it the best I could, and the rumors were fading away until the accident revived them. I'd hoped by coming here, I could escape the constant, morbid surveillance by the media.''

Catching her breath, she gave Grady a sidelong glance and awaited his reaction.

''Hmm,'' was all he said as he contemplated her explanation.

She restrained herself from screaming in frustration.

For the next hour, Kate felt like the unwilling star of a television mystery movie. First, she and Grady went back to her parents' house. Grady instructed Ollie to wait on the porch. Tension filled the living room when Grady and Hewett Sparks came face-to-face, exchanging cold hellos. No doubt Sparks had heard talk about Grady running against him and saw Grady as his opposition's ringleader. And Grady probably thought if Sparks had been doing his job, people wouldn't be pressuring him to do something he didn't want to do.

As Kate began her hurried explanation, every face in the room narrowed with concern.

"Is there anything we can do, dear?" Evie offered.

"Just don't tell anyone where I am." She didn't know the Sparkses that well, but she had to trust them to keep her secret.

Eva turned to her husband. "Can't you have the police check on this man, Hewett? A stranger here shouldn't be hard to find."

Hewett shrugged his ample shoulders. "They can't make him leave. There's no law against his just being here."

"There are laws against stalking," Julia replied stiffly.

A shiver raced up Kate's spine. "I can't prove he's following me. I'm not even sure it was the same man both times."

"Both times?" Julia asked, her eyebrows flaring. "You've seen him before tonight?"

Kate shifted uneasily. The last thing she wanted was to cause her parents more worry. "In the parking lot behind Vine's," she said quickly. "But it was probably just someone on his way downtown." Her glance swung briefly to Grady, meeting his gaze. Funny, she thought, that she had nearly forgotten that part of the incident but she vividly remembered Grady had been about to kiss her. Was he thinking of that now too?

"I've got to pack some clothes," she excused herself.

"I'll get some groceries together," Julia volunteered, rushing to the kitchen, shaking her head as she walked. "I really don't like this."

Kate followed her mother into the kitchen. "It's either this or go back to New York," Kate told her.

Julia gave her daughter a hug. "Of course I want you here for Christmas. But out at the lake all alone?"

"Just to throw this reporter offtrack. I'll be in and out of town. I'll be fine, Mom. I'm not afraid of being alone."

A hand clasped her shoulder, and she looked up to see Grady standing beside her. "And I'll make sure she's all right, Mrs. Smithers," he promised.

Half an hour later, she was back in Grady's Explorer, staring out the window as they twisted down the winding country road.

"I didn't realize your parents and the Sparkses were friends," he said.

"Neither did I," Kate replied, studying his profile in the darkness. His strong jaw was now set in a familiar, determined manner. "I'll do everything it takes to get him out of the mayor's office, even if it comes down to running myself."

"He says he's not running for reelection. His son isn't running either."

"Really?"

"From his side, what's been happening here isn't all his fault."

"Of course, he'd say that."

"Grady, give him a chance."

"Do you believe him?"

"There's probably some truth to what he's saying."

"He's had chances for the past twenty years. This has always been a hick town, but it just doesn't feel right anymore. People aren't calm and friendly like they used to be."

"Sounds like a campaign speech to me."

"Well, after all, you're just visiting. I'm sure it's easy for you to see everything we're doing wrong here. There's more to consider for those of us who have commitments."

Kate fell silent.

After several seconds, Grady glanced sideways at her. "I'm sorry. I guess deep down inside there's a little demon that still resents your leaving."

"You didn't ask me to stay, Grady."

"How could I have? Would it have made any difference?"

"I don't know. How can I say now what I would have done years ago? I know I would have wanted to."

"For what it's worth, I kept hoping you'd change

your mind. I even sometimes hoped you'd fail and come running home.''

Kate's voice dropped.

''Oh, Grady.''

''Funny how life works sometimes. I stayed here to help my family out when Kenny was sick, and until I decided to open my clinic in Shady Pointe, I didn't realize I'd always wanted to stay.''

''But we talked all the time about moving away.''

''That was part of a different dream. That was about the two of us together. After you were in New York becoming so successful, the punch had gone out of it.''

''You would have gone on my account?''

''Back then, I'd convinced myself that was what I wanted to do.''

''Maybe what happened was for the best. I wouldn't want uprooting you on my conscience.'' He was right. She couldn't imagine him being happy away from here.

He grinned. ''I might have found a place I liked better. Right now, a tropical climate sounds good.''

''White sandy beaches, crystal-blue calm water, warm breezes rustling the palm trees,'' she agreed. Then she flushed, realizing she'd been envisioning the two of them there together.

''Perfect,'' Grady replied, and she wondered if his mental picture included her or someone else.

Kate dug teeth into her lower lip. ''What about Libby? Will you ask her to stay?'' she blurted.

He cast her a strained glance but didn't answer.

Kate stared down at her hands, aghast that she'd pried into his intentions about Libby. The words had poured out on their own. Why did she so desperately need to know where he and Libby stood? It couldn't possibly make any difference. She wondered why he'd bothered asking about that silly mixup with Hall. The man hadn't even particularly impressed her.

The last few minutes of the ride passed in silence— her punishment for intruding, she supposed. He didn't owe her any explanations.

She was relieved when he pulled the truck up to the cabin. As he'd warned, it was a plain frame box.

''I'm still working on it,'' he explained as he un-loaded her suitcases.

''You built this yourself?'' she asked.

''Don't worry, I had help from my dad. It won't cave in on you.''

''I didn't think it would,'' she countered, reaching for the box of groceries her mom had packed.

Ollie pranced happily through the snow.

She glanced toward the frozen lake, the pristine snowscape shimmering in the moonlight. The world was so still, she could nearly hear her own heartbeat.

''It's beautiful out here,'' she reflected.

Grady smiled. ''And quiet. If I ever get this place finished, I plan to live out here full-time.'' He stood just over her shoulder. She felt the heat of him behind her.

She laughed lightly. "I don't even know where you live now."

"I'm renting an old farmhouse just outside town. It's close to the clinic and there's open space for Ollie. I can show it to you sometime if you'd like . . ." His voice dropped off suddenly. "Let's go inside. It's too cold to stand out here," he finished without giving her a chance to answer.

The cabin's interior was modest, but the structure was roomier inside than she'd expected. The smells of lumber and paint lingered. In here, there was no escaping Grady or thoughts of him. He'd put too much of himself into this place.

"This is wonderful, Grady," she said, setting her box on the square wooden kitchen table.

"Most of the furnishings are my parents' castoffs. At least there's heat. Let me go turn it up."

"I'm sure Libby will have suggestions for decorating it."

He gave her another hard, cold stare. This one chilled her blood. Why did she have to keep bringing up Libby? Talk about inner demons.

Mercifully, he ignored her comment. "What did you bring to eat? I'm starved."

"I don't know. I'm sure my mom probably stuffed her whole week's worth of groceries in here." She sifted through the box's contents. "How does a ham

sandwich and vegetable soup sound?'' she asked finally.

''Great. Something we can fix quickly. The draw-
back to being Santa is there's no dinner break.''

''I was on my way to get a hamburger when you
picked me up. From Baker's.''

''They're the best, aren't they? I must have eaten a
thousand of those greasy things. Mom was always telling us not to eat them, and my brothers and I would
sneak off whenever we had extra money.''

While she located a pan to heat the soup in, he hung
his coat on the back of the kitchen chair and began
making sandwiches.

It surprised her how easily they worked together,
but then it shouldn't have. It felt almost like old times
when they'd cook a meal or a snack side-by-side in
one of their kitchens on Apple Blossom Drive. Pre-
paring food was the one thing Grady had never been
much good at, but he always tried.

Throughout the meal, she refrained from bringing
up Libby again.

''Your cooking has improved,'' she decreed, holding up the sandwich.

A corner of his mouth curled. ''Not much,'' he admitted.

Kate flashed him a warm smile, then quickly returned her attention to her food.

''Are you sure you're going to be all right out
here?'' Grady asked.

"Sure," she answered. "You know I will."

He smiled appreciatively. "Yes, I should be pitying that reporter if he catches up with you. In any case, I'm leaving Ollie to protect you."

Kate eyed the huge animal sprawled beside the table. "Must you?" she asked warily.

"I'll feel better if I do. Will you be all right with him? If you want him to mind, you have to sound stern. At least he'll bark if anyone comes around."

She reached down and patted the canine's head. "We'll manage," she assured him. "But I don't have any dog food."

"I'll be back early tomorrow, so we can exchange vehicles. I'll bring his food and his heartworm pills and his toys."

"Why do I suddenly feel like I'm baby-sitting?" she asked. "I thought he was supposed to be guarding *me*."

Disappointment prodded her as Grady reached for his coat. Silly, she thought. She couldn't have expected him to stay long, but she realized she didn't want him to go.

"I'll be back first thing in the morning," he promised. "You've got your phone, right? Just call if you need anything." He reached in his wallet and took out a business card. "This has my home number on it. Is there anything special you need me to bring?"

She shook her head. Her fingers brushed his as she took the card. He was standing over her so close she suddenly felt as skittish as a fireman on the Fourth of July.

He hesitated before leaving, studying her.

''Why are you so anxious to push me and Libby together, Katie?'' he asked.

She frowned nervously. ''I just assumed you and she . . .''

''Would you feel safer then about what you're feeling?'' he asked.

Her eyebrows shot up. How did he presume to know what she was feeling when she didn't herself?

He didn't wait for her to answer. ''At least I'm honest enough to admit I'm still feeling something for you. I don't know what it is, but I think you're feeling something too. Considering how close we were once, it's perfectly natural. Maybe if we just talked it out instead of dancing around it.''

Kate folded her arms. ''There's nothing to discuss. I'll always be fond of you, Grady, and I want you to be happy. That's all. Libby seems very nice.''

He stared at her for what felt like several minutes before marching to the door.

''Good night, Katie,'' he said distractedly, his eyes scanning the surrounding woods.

So, she thought, that's why he'd lingered, to make sure no one had followed them.

She jumped at the sound of the door slamming behind him.

''Good night, Grady,'' she murmured.

Chapter Eight

Lulled by the fresh country air, Kate slept better that night than she anticipated. Ollie stretched out on the floor alongside the wood frame bed, and she was happy to have his silent companionship. Well, nearly silent. Just before she drifted off to sleep, she heard the steady roll of his snoring. *The ever-alert watchdog,* she thought with a drowsy smile.

When she awoke, she found the cabin quiet, sunshine spilling through the front window. In robe and slippers, she padded to the front room and absorbed the panoramic view of the lake. So this was Grady's world.

Thinking of his angry departure last night, she shifted uneasily. She was doing the best thing for both of them. What good would it do to profess feelings she could never follow through on? Why did he insist on trying to provoke her into doing exactly that? He probably expected her to acknowledge she harbored a mild degree of sentimental attachment to him. After all, he had been her first love. He was probably hoping merely to put their old relationship in its proper perspective. It was just like Grady to need to analyze everything. But he couldn't know she'd never felt as much for anyone else, that she was beginning to doubt she ever would. Oh, he'd be reeling if she revealed the deep stirrings she was feeling for him now, wishing he'd left it alone. What good would admitting them do? Make him feel guilty because his feelings had faded and he'd fallen for someone else? No, she had to leave him free to get on with his life without worrying about her.

Still, now that she was staying in his cabin, she couldn't avoid thoughts of him. And Grady had always had a way of wrenching the truth out of her.

She knew Grady's impatience with her last night wouldn't stop him from coming back today as he'd promised. Besides, she had his dog. Who was now tap dancing frantically in front of the door.

"All right," she told Ollie, meeting his pleading gaze and unlatching the lock. "I wasn't thinking. I'm not used to having an animal in the house."

She opened the door, and he bolted out. "Don't go

too far,'' she called after him. She and Grady were on thin ice as it was without her having to explain losing his dog.

Closing the door, she found coffee in the kitchen and set up the coffeemaker. As the liquid brewed, she washed up and dressed in leggings and a tunic sweater. The outfit was casual and comfortable, but fairly new. She'd chosen it because the royal blue top set off her coloring so nicely. Pausing, she glimpsed her reflection in the mirror.

Taken aback, she studied the stranger staring at her. Magically, the life had slipped back into her face. In the past months, she'd grown accustomed to seeing a thin, pale, worried expression. Today, her cheeks were full and rosy; her blue eyes sparkled with silver. How had that happened?

Impulsively, she applied a smidgen of powder and eye shadow and lip gloss to bring out her coloring.

Satisfied, she tucked the cosmetics back into her cloth pouch. She looked almost human again. And knowing that made her feel stronger somehow. If she was beginning to look good, maybe she'd start feeling good again. Like she used to. In the past few months she'd continued her usual careful grooming out of habit. But deep down she hadn't really cared whether she'd looked attractive or not.

Still, she couldn't help wondering if her inner glow this morning came from knowing she'd be seeing

Grady. No, she couldn't allow herself to get her fragile emotions tangled up with him.

The knock on the door startled her.

Rushing to open it, she found Grady and Ollie awaiting her.

"Hi!" she greeted Grady cheerfully, hoping they could forget last night. She stepped aside so he could enter.

"Hi!" he replied incredulously, drawing up beside her and staring down at her. "Why so chipper this morning? I expected you'd be miserable and complaining about the crude accommodations. But this place seems to agree with you. You look . . . different."

"I'll assume that's a compliment. I love it here, Grady," she blurted. "Ollie and I slept like logs. I didn't know dogs snored."

Grady chuckled. "I should have warned you about Ollie's annoying habit. One of many, I'm afraid. Is that coffee I smell?"

"Want some? I'm afraid I slept in."

"I'm not in any hurry."

She filled two mugs with coffee. Grady sat in a worn armchair near the window. Kate remembered the chair from his parents' living room. Long ago, it had been placed near the hearth. Grady's dad always used to sit in it when he first got home from work.

"Are you sure you don't mind my staying here, Grady?" she asked.

"No, I don't mind. Why?"

"After last night, I just thought you might prefer my being somewhere else."

"Forget it. Maybe I was just trying to get you to say something you don't feel. I was out of line."

"No, *I* was. I didn't mean to keep bringing up Libby. I shouldn't have. Your relationship with her is none of my business."

She realized she'd been hoping he'd say he didn't love the pretty teacher. Her foolish heart sank when he changed the subject. "Did you bring your boots?"

"Of course."

"I just wondered, you were tromping around in those little sneakers yesterday."

"That was accidental."

"Put your boots on. I want to show you something."

"What?"

"It's a surprise. I can't describe it."

Following his instructions, she bundled up in boots, coat, and scarf. Outside, he led her into the woods.

"How far are we going?" she asked.

"Not far," he replied cryptically. She struggled to keep from slipping as the trail led them downhill.

"Grady Meredith, have you lost your mind?" she called finally.

"Just a few feet farther."

Momentarily, he stopped, and she slid into his back. He reached behind him to brace her.

"Look," he said, pointing.

Hearing a gurgling sound, she leaned down and saw the spring. He leaned close beside her, and she felt the heat of his skin on her face.

"It's not frozen?" she asked.

"I've never seen it freeze."

"You brought me all the way out here to show me this?"

"It flows into a creek farther down. Do you want to go on, or are you ready to turn back?"

"Let's go," she said. She hated his treating her like a fragile figurine and he knew it. She began to believe he was being intentionally solicitous just to irritate her. This whole outing was some kind of test. Summer or winter, she could hike just as far through the woods as he could.

His asking three times whether she was tired proved her theory. Finally, they arrived at the creek. Grady leaned against a crooked tree.

Kate set her hands on her hips, about to accuse him of leading her on a futile expedition, but she saw he was staring at the creek and not paying her a bit of attention. Suddenly, she looked around and grasped the beauty of their surroundings—the snow-laden banks, the twisting bare tree branches overhead. The only sound she heard was the rushing water. The world was frozen, waiting beneath the ice and snow to come alive once again in spring. And she thought perhaps her heart had endured its winter, waiting to bloom once again . . .

"It's breathtaking," she conceded, dropping her defensive pose. "I could stay here forever."

"Maybe now you can understand why I'm not wild about the possibility of a developer moving in here."

"Of course, I understand. But it would be good for Shady Pointe. If the city works with the developer to ensure it's done properly, with certain regulations enforced, the environment doesn't have to be compromised. There's a lot of open land here, and the town so desperately needs something to reassure people life here can be good."

He gave her an inquisitive look. "I had no idea you had such deep concern for the town's welfare."

"Even though I haven't lived here for a long time, my roots are still here. It hurts to see everyone unhappy and complaining."

"It's not all Sparks' fault," he admitted. "Nothing's been the same here since the clothing factory closed down a few years ago. I suppose he's taken the brunt of the blame for the hard times."

Kate scanned the snowscape before her. "I've been here before. With you, Grady." Strong emotions she didn't understand surfaced inside her.

He faced her, his eyes darkening to near black. "I wondered if you'd recognize it. It was summer then."

"Before I left," she added. "You used to sneak out here and fish in the creek all the time. But you'd told me you never brought anyone out here before because it was the only place where you knew you could be alone.''

"And I haven't since."

Her lips puckered into a puzzled circle. "Why did you bring me here?''

"Since you're staying at the cabin, I thought you should know the way. I always feel peaceful after I've been out here for a while. I just thought you might need some space of your own right now.''

A lump clogged her throat, and hot tears pooled in the corners of her eyes. Suddenly, Kate understood the impact this place was having on her. Until now, it was the last time they'd been alone together. She'd been young and so full of vitality and optimism. "That was the day you told me about Kenny. That you'd decided to stay. You broke my heart.''

Her last words slid out on their own. She hadn't meant to reveal so much.

He reached out and brushed the hair from the side of her face. "No one could have held you back. I wanted so much to take care of you, but you never could accept that. Oh, I know you're capable of managing on your own. That's not the way I mean. At the time, I thought we'd go on feeling the same way about each other forever.''

Kate blinked back threatening tears. All the emotions she'd tucked so neatly away surfaced, as raw as a bruise. But she refused to cry in front of him. "Don't do this, Grady,'' she pleaded. ''We always watched out for each other. Everything changes. We've changed.''

He stepped closer, snow crunching beneath his boots.

''We're not kids anymore. I think it's time we stopped pretending we are.''

''I can't. It's too hard.''

''Nothing is too hard, Katie. I know you've always believed that—except when it came to us. I don't understand.''

''I'm not the same person you knew, Grady. I don't want to disappoint you. Can't we just leave the past behind us? None of it matters anymore.''

He reached up, scooping her face in both hands, holding it up to meet his as though examining a great prize. His fingers traced the fine line of her jaw.

His gentle, tentative touch shot warm ripples down her neck. Tenderness welled inside her as she looked into those rich, compelling eyes. All she wanted was to be wrapped in his arms. She couldn't think of anything else.

''I think it does matter.''

''Oh, Grady,'' she whispered, tears stinging her eyes. She'd never dreamed she'd ever be able to be this close to him again. And for this moment, she couldn't deny the tug on her heart, no matter what the warning signals in her head were telling her.

He silenced her by running a fingertip across her

lips. As he bowed his head, she leaned forward, finding his lips as they fell over hers, as sweet and magical as she remembered.

His strong arms enveloped her, and she relinquished herself to their comfort. Her heart was racing, and she felt more alive than she had since the accident, her emotions bubbling, the air colder and crisper, the sky bluer.

Dazed by the overwhelming onrush of emotions she feared she would lose control of completely, she reluctantly drew back from him.

She raked splayed fingertips through her hair, turning away. "No, I'm sorry. This is wrong. We could never be right for each other."

"Are we so wrong for each other then?"

She couldn't look at him. "I'm only here for a short while. I'd hate to see a little nostalgia ruin the rest of your life."

"Nostalgia?" he asked. "Nostalgia is an old song on the radio or looking through the high school yearbook. There's more than that going on here."

Her hands balled into nervous fists. "We both have other priorities," she said, her voice quavering.

His eyebrows arched. "Is this about Libby?" he asked. "Because . . ."

She was shaking her head sadly. "No, Grady. It's about me."

A shadow crossed his expression. "We'd better be getting back," he said evenly, turning and heading up the path. Kate was glad to walk behind him, where he couldn't see the rogue tears that spilled down her cheeks.

By the time they'd reached the cabin, she'd composed herself.

Grady turned to her solemnly. ''That van was in front of your parents' house this morning. We can try to switch vehicles, but if he starts following you, we'll have to think of something else.''

Kate nodded stiffly, unable to meet his eyes. ''All right. I can't stay out here without a car. I have things to do.''

Grady whistled for Ollie, who bounded obediently to his side. He patted the dog's head absently.

During the drive back to town, Grady turned on the radio, and the soft drone of Christmas carols relieved them of the need to make conversation. But Kate studied him surreptitiously as he drove. She'd never known anyone as honest and intelligent and compassionate as Grady. He cared so much about the world around him—people, animals, the environment. She'd always admired him for it. All the effervescence he'd inspired in her was still there, but what she felt for him now surpassed her burning teenage crush. She'd matured enough, had lost enough, to understand what love was about. And she knew she'd had more reason to distance herself from him than selfishness. Grady had never given her the one thing she'd needed most—he'd never admitted that he needed her—and she hadn't been willing to settle for having him on his terms.

And that was why she couldn't permit herself to love him now. And why she could do nothing that might interfere in his relationship with Libby. Maybe Libby was the woman he really loved after all.

Considering that made her feel empty inside.

Suffocating from the tension, she was relieved when they reached her parents' house.

Julia greeted her with a hug. The house smelled of roasting meat and spices.

"I fixed dinner. You and Grady can stay long enough to eat, can't you?" she asked.

Kate shifted her eyes questioningly toward Grady. He was probably anxious to get her back to the cabin so he could eat with his folks, as he usually did on Sundays.

"Sure," he answered. "Whatever you're cooking smells delicious."

He drifted into the living room where Kate's dad was watching a football game, and dropped into a chair.

Volunteering to help with the food, Kate followed her mom into the kitchen.

"Is everything really all right?" Julia asked when they were alone. "You weren't afraid being alone at the lake?"

"I wasn't totally alone. Grady left his dog with me."

Julia's brow wrinkled into a deep V. "The one that almost attacked you?"

Kate laughed lightly. "We just misunderstood each other. He's out on the porch right now."

Julia assessed her critically. "Well, something out there must agree with you. Your eyes look brighter than they have since you got here."

Kate pinched a carrot stick from the relish tray. "I suppose I didn't realize that just because I wasn't physically damaged, I didn't still need time to heal. I expected to go back to the way I was right away. And not being able to do that was frustrating."

Julia moved a pot off the stove. "I'm happy to see you're feeling better. But I know that means you'll be leaving soon."

"Mom, you and Dad never held me back from anything I wanted to accomplish. You always allowed me the freedom to find out on my own what I wanted to do, even when it sounded crazy. I'm sorry that my ventures have kept us so far apart. When I leave again, I'll be back to visit more often."

Julia sighed.

"What's wrong, Mom?"

"I was hoping Grady might have changed your mind about leaving. You two were always so crazy about each other."

"Back in high school. That's not going to happen, Mom." She carried a stack of dishes into the dining room.

Dinner wasn't as strained as Kate expected. Grady chatted easily with her parents. While he included her in the conversation, she noticed he avoided looking at her. Julia's pot roast and mashed potatoes might as well have been charcoal and paste for all Kate tasted her food.

She should never have weakened and fallen into Grady's arms. He suspected the truth now, and he was angry at her for denying it.

Well, he'd just have to stay angry.

Kate tried to take an active role in the discussion. "Will there be the community caroling the night before Christmas Eve?" she asked brightly, tearing a roll. "I think I've missed that more than anything in this town."

No one answered right away.

Kate wondered what she had said that was wrong.

"Mabel Osgood and some of her friends are organizing a boycott," Grady finally muttered.

"Boycotting Christmas carols?" she asked incredulously. "This town sure has gone to the wolves."

"It's a protest against Hewett Sparks and his dirty politics."

"Maybe Mabel would do better to sit down and talk to him instead of getting the whole town stirred up."

"And ruining everyone's holiday," Julia added.

"I don't plan to go," Grady said.

Kate saw her father's complexion grow purplish. That half the town was at odds with the other half was bad enough without a political debate breaking out at the dinner table. Nothing like an old-fashioned hometown Christmas.

"That's ridiculous," she shot back. "Christmas is a time for people to come together. You'll only be making a bad situation worse."

"I'm sure Grady has his reasons," Julia defended him.

"Please, could we talk about something else?" Kate requested.

All three turned to her, and for a long moment silence hung over the table. Then Grady brought up the latest weather forecast, restoring the easy flow of conversation. No more snow was expected, at least for the next day or two.

Kate shot him a grateful glance. She felt plenty of tension between the two of them without arguing over politics. After dinner, he insisted on helping Julia clear the table while Kate went upstairs to collect more of her belongings. Impulsively, she stuck a couple of her old dolls in the suitcase and decided to take her portable sewing machine and sewing box, both of which she'd unearthed in the attic.

As she descended the stairs, wrestling to hold her heavy baggage, she heard Grady's voice from the kitchen. "There's nothing to keep her here. In a way, I'll be relieved when she does go."

She stood at the bottom of the stairs, indignant and betrayed. Grady and her mother were discussing her!

But his words were what chilled her heart. Despite his claims of lingering affection, his kiss this afternoon, he wanted her to go. Perhaps having her gone would be a relief to everyone.

Unfortunately, the heavy suitcase slipped out of her hand, clunking as it hit the step and bounced onto the floor.

Kate stood amid a rush of footsteps headed to the hall.

"Are you all right?" Julia asked.

"I just dropped a suitcase," she said, struggling to set the machine and sewing box down so she could retrieve it.

Grady took the bulky objects from her hands. "Why didn't you tell someone you needed help?" he asked.

She cast him a sour look. "I thought I could manage," she countered.

"All this?" he asked incredulously.

"I'd just about made it," she protested. And she would have if he hadn't been in the kitchen talking about her, she reflected.

He set her things down on the floor and went to the front window.

"That van is still there," he reported.

"You think the reporter's in there?" Kate's father asked.

"He came out of it last night," Grady told him.

Kate rubbed her chin. "We'll have to distract him."

"Good idea," Grady agreed. "How?"

"Dad can call Mr. Sparks. He can send over a police car to check out the suspicious vehicle. That's when we'll leave."

Grady's expression told her he didn't approve of involving Sparks. But he admitted he couldn't come up with anything better.

While Norman Smithers was on the phone, she and Grady nonchalantly carried her things out to the Explorer. Then they went back inside, watching out the window until the blue-and-white police cruiser pulled up across the street.

She dashed into his Explorer, taking Ollie with her, and Grady got into her BMW. She backed out of the driveway, heading west. Grady came out next, turning east. As planned, they were taking different routes to reach the highway that went to the lake.

Feeling like a bank robber making a getaway, Kate smiled victoriously as she headed the highway and found no one behind her except Grady in her car.

She jumped out of the truck nearly as quickly as Ollie did after arriving at the cabin. In the excitement, she'd nearly forgotten the tension between her and Grady.

But Grady's grim expression told her he hadn't.

He carried her baggage inside, and she realized now that she had transportation, he had no need to return while she was here.

"Does all this remind you of playing cops and robbers as a kid?" she asked.

The shadow of a smile crossed his expression. "Yes, but like you said, we're not kids anymore. And this is too real for my liking. He's invading your privacy."

He turned to leave. "Aren't you going to take Ollie?" she asked.

He tossed her keys in the air, then caught them. "I'll feel better about your being out here if I know he's with you. The two of you seem to be getting along all right. Besides, you don't want him dancing around in the backseat of your nice clean car."

"I suppose not," she agreed. "If you miss him, you can come and visit."

He gave her a long, hard look. "I'll be back," was all he said.

Chapter Nine

Kate spent the rest of the afternoon scrubbing her
old dolls and sketching costume ideas. She'd hoped
the activity would stop her from wondering where
Grady had gone and how he'd spent the rest of his
day. But as hard as she tried, she couldn't erase her
mental picture of his going straight to Libby, express-
ing regret that seeing to Kate's welfare had been taking up so much of his time, apologizing for the need
to help a stubborn old friend.

She pushed the vision away, knowing she had no
right to resent his finding happiness with someone better suited for him. After all, Grady had always known
what he needed.

As the early dusk shrouded the windows, she

paused to heat soup, then scooped it from a mug as she worked. Except for the scratching of her pencil, Ollie's rhythmic snoring, and the hum of the refrigerator, the cabin was quiet.

She continued drawing until her eyelids felt heavy. Carefully packing away her drawing materials, she took a hot, leisurely shower and dressed in a flannel gown and a robe. Idly, she curled up on the sofa, scanning the Sunday paper her mother had insisted she bring from the house. She let Ollie out, hoping he wouldn't decide to run off. She could just imagine herself chasing after him in her slippers and wet hair. Fortunately, he was back scratching at the door ten minutes later.

Locking the doors and turning out the lights, she went to bed. As soon as she closed her eyes, she saw Grady's handsome, familiar face. Sadness welled up inside her. There was no escaping him here. Even the prints on the wall depicting wooded landscapes and majestic wild animals brought him to mind. She loved him, would always love him, even if they could never be together. She'd learned a long time ago life wasn't fair. But despite everything, she kept hoping just once fate would right itself. Until now, she'd always been able to see light even in the darkest night. When she walked away from Grady this time, it would be the hardest thing she'd ever done, because she knew this time it was for good. And yet she had to do it. If only she could care less, leaving would be easier. Besides, he wanted her to go.

Finally, she fell asleep, waking early to find Ollie settled on the bed, lying on his side with his spine pressed against her legs.

"Get down!" she ordered, laughing at his audacity.

Startled, Ollie rose, stepping all over her in the process of jumping down. He glanced back, flashing indignant brown eyes.

"Monster," she muttered, still giggling. She hoped he didn't have fleas. She shook the quilt and brushed it with one hand.

Boosting herself to the edge of the bed, she stuffed her feet into her comfortable old mules and shuffled to the front door to let him out.

The morning had dawned sunny and clear, casting a blinding sheen on the snow-covered ground. The air smelled cold and damp and sweet. After Ollie raced into the woods, Kate stood for a minute with the door open, leaning against the door frame and inhaling deeply. The small joys such as this, that made her feel right again for odd moments, reaffirmed that her life went on for a reason. If only she could find a way to freeze her fleeting contentment.

After setting up the coffeemaker, she dressed in jeans and a sweater. She brushed her hair until it curled softly over her shoulders, then carefully applied a small amount of makeup. As she leaned in front of the mirror, she realized she was primping in hopes Grady would come today.

She heard Ollie pawing at the door. Rushing to let him in, she served him his dog food in the kitchen, then scrambled an egg and made toast for herself. She washed the dishes, including Ollie's, setting them in the drainer to dry, then looked around for something else to do.

On such a bright day, bristling with anticipation, she felt restless being shut up in the cabin. Or maybe she just wanted to escape a place that reminded her so much of Grady.

Donning her coat and boots, she took Ollie outside with her. She walked along the lakeshore and was lost in her thoughts when she discovered the hulking dog was no longer at her side.

"Ollie?" she called, alarmed when he did not reappear.

She glanced worriedly at the thin coating of ice over the edge of the lake. A dog without any sense might go prancing onto it. A dog the size of a pony might crash through the ice and drown.

"Ollie!" she called more loudly.

He wasn't exactly her best friend, but she didn't want any harm to come to him. She remembered how Grady had whistled for him, but she never had been able to whistle.

"Ollie!"

Frantically, she scanned the lake and the shore, seeing no sign of him.

Then she felt a nudge at her backside. Whirling, she found Ollie staring up at her quizzically, as though he couldn't imagine what he'd done wrong.

"You dim-witted beast," she scolded, shaking a finger at him. "Don't do that!"

His head bobbed up and down as his eyes followed her finger.

Kate groaned in exasperation. Then, realizing how glad she was to find him unscathed, she burst into laughter, bending to hug the big animal around the neck.

"Come on," she told him. "And you stay where I can see you. Grady will be awfully mad if I don't take proper care of you."

Halting, she wondered whether Grady had left the dog not so much for protection as to force her to concentrate on something outside herself.

Darn Grady. She could go to New York, Zimbabwe, the Yukon, and never be free of him.

Maybe it was time to face up to that instead of hiding from it. Struck by an impulse, she searched for a familiar landmark to locate the path they'd taken yesterday. Finally, she found it, following the hard-packed snow past the spring to the creek—Grady's place. His boot tracks remained imprinted in the snow.

She leaned against the same tree he'd propped himself against yesterday, closing her eyes and feeling the

cold air against her cheeks as she listened to the bab-
bling water. Recalling the image of Grady close before
her, she didn't struggle to push it away. She could
almost feel his presence here. For the first time, she
allowed all her buried feelings for him to surface.

At first, it was unsettling. An overwhelming, bitter-
sweet sadness welled inside her, rising slowly to the
surface. A thick lump clogged her throat, and tears
stung her eyes. She thought of all the days she'd gotten out of bed, gone about her routine, arrived at her
office, taking her life for granted and believing it
would always be the same. She'd taken love for
granted as well, believing she'd found it once and
would find it again. Well, she had found it again. But
it was here in Shady Pointe with Grady. She had to
face facts. In her lifetime, she would love only one
man. No one would measure up to Grady.

Could she let him go on believing all she felt was
a chummy affection? Could she let him marry Libby
without admitting she loved him?

Maybe she was more afraid than noble. Afraid she'd
waited too long, that he loved Libby and would marry
her anyway. Maybe Libby was the one he needed in
his life, and she couldn't compete with that.

She remembered him digging into his pocket for the
little boy at the community center. For Grady, giving
came easily. He'd grown up in a large, close-knit family bound into an even tighter circle when Kenny was
sick. Grady was accustomed to taking charge of the

people he cared about. Kate had grown up an only child in a more reserved family. Sharing what was in her heart had always come harder, slower. But when she drew someone close to her, it was for keeps.

Now, accepting the reality of her love for Grady made her feel stronger. If she could still love, she could go on with her life. She realized her life would never revert to exactly what it was before the accident. The experience, the loss, had changed her forever. She would never view life exactly the same way again. But it didn't make her any less human, any less Kate Smithers than she'd been six months or a year ago. That too was something she had to accept.

She sighed deeply. Alone in these isolated woods, she was aware of the essence of herself. A fire burned inside her that no tragedy could take away. She had to stop being afraid. If her life had been spared for a reason, it wasn't for her to cower inside her parents' house, but rather to cherish the chance to take risks, to be willing to lose everything and know that she could fail and still be true to herself.

Her feelings for Grady were a part of her. In denying them, she was making herself feel less than normal.

She attempted a feeble whistle and was astounded when Ollie trotted obediently to her side. Absently, she rubbed his head.

She walked slowly back to the cabin, hoping to glimpse her own car as she crested the hill.

But it wasn't there. Grady hadn't come.

Throughout the rest of the day, she waited, her heart twisting every time she thought she heard a vehicle nearing. But no visitors came. She could have called him, but she had no legitimate reason to request his presence. If he was staying away, it was because he wanted to.

She occupied herself with her dolls and flitted restlessly about the cabin. As night fell, she gave up on expecting him. When she lay sleeplessly in the bed, covered by his mother's patchwork quilt, she feared she had waited too long to admit the truth. Perhaps Grady felt so free to admit he felt something between them only because he felt so much less.

Kate awoke early again on Tuesday morning, immediately remembering her promise to visit Libby's class today. She was torn between looking forward to having something useful to do and dreading facing the perky young woman who'd captured Grady's heart.

Determined not to be beaten down by her emotions, she showered and dressed. Realizing she hadn't brought any appropriate clothing, she put on jeans and a sweater, thinking she'd stop at her parents' house and change. She curled her hair with electric rollers, pulling the top section back into a wooden barrette and letting the curls sweep over her neck and shoulders.

As long as she had to go into town, she'd have a chance to finish her Christmas shopping. Only a few days remained before the holiday, and she had something special in mind she wanted to get, if she could find it.

When she reached her parents' house, she was disappointed to find they weren't home. Her mother had supplied her with a spare key, so getting inside was no problem. She went upstairs and found what she was seeking—her camel-color wool suit and a white shirt. She changed clothes and tied a paisley scarf around her collar. As she was straightening the scarf, the doorbell rang.

Deciding it must be someone looking for her parents, she tried to ignore it. But it rang a second and then a third time, and finally, squelching a trace of annoyance at the intrusion, she marched downstairs.

Noel stood on the doorstep, blond hair blowing across his forehead, an angry frown slashing his face.

"Noel!" she greeted him. "What's wrong? My parents aren't here right now."

"You're the one I'm looking for, Kate. Where have you been? Nobody would tell me where you'd run off to."

Kate studied him thoughtfully. She'd assumed her parents and Grady were the only people who needed to know her whereabouts. She hadn't dreamed Noel might be concerned, or that anyone might refuse to tell him where she was.

"I'm sorry, Noel. Come on in, and I'll explain."

Still looking chagrined, he grudgingly stepped inside.

"Have a seat," she offered, gesturing toward the living room.

After sweeping his glance around the room, he dropped down on the sofa. "What's going on, Kate? I keep calling, and your parents say you're out. I saw Grady getting coffee in the Sandwich Works this morning, and he told me you'd gone off to some undisclosed location to be alone. Then I was driving by and saw his Explorer in the driveway. What gives?"

As understanding set in, Kate drew in a sharp breath. "I've been staying at Grady's cabin at Echo Lake. It is a secret, but not one you can't be in on. Grady and I traded vehicles because a reporter was following me."

Noel's expression slackened, but Kate saw anger still burning in his eyes.

"A reporter?" He rubbed his jaw. "I thought you were avoiding me."

"I'd never do that. I'm sorry for the misunderstanding. It's my fault. I made everyone promise not to disclose my whereabouts. I didn't stop to consider you might be looking for me."

He studied the carpet, then swung his glance up to meet hers. "I suppose that says a lot about where you and I stand. I thought we'd been getting along pretty well. I guess I've never gotten over that crush I used to have on you. I was hoping at this point the difference in our ages wouldn't matter anymore.''

Kate's mouth formed a small circle. She remembered Grady's tongue-in-cheek warning about Noel at the Dunmores' party. At the time, she'd dismissed it, believing Grady was only goading her. But he'd picked up on something she'd missed. Maybe she'd been too self-absorbed to see Noel was offering more than friendship. And now she'd disappointed him without meaning to.

''Noel, when you came out of your parents' house the other night, I was feeling jittery about going to the party at all. I was about to run back here when you dragged me inside. You made it easy to lean on you when I needed some propping up. You made me laugh at a point when I needed to more than anything. I enjoy being with you, and I didn't intend to use you. I thought we were friends.''

''Well, now that we've got that straightened out, will you go out with me again? I could drive out to the cabin.''

She shook her head. ''That's not a good idea.''

''I'm not that much younger than you. I'll be finished with med school in a few years.''

''It's not because of our ages. I think that's why I felt so safe with you and your friends. All of you reminded me of better days, easier times.''

''Then it's Grady, isn't it?''

She shook her head. ''Noel, I've always thought of

you with the type of affection I'd have for a little brother or a cousin. Even when we're both old, I'll feel that way.''

"I knew it when I saw the way you and Grady looked at each other at my folks' party.''

She wrung her hands in her lap. "Noel, this has nothing to do with Grady. Besides, he seems pretty settled with Libby, and I'll just have to accept that.''

"I hate to shatter your illusions, but Chelsea says Libby's landed a teaching job back in her hometown. She's not even coming back after Christmas break.''

Kate gasped, raising fingertips to her mouth. "She's leaving?''

"From what I hear, she never cared much for Shady Pointe. And the woman's not blind. Anyone can see you and Grady are wild about each other. Anyone except you and Grady, I guess. I'd been hoping that was over, but since you're not going to allow me to sweep you out of your boots, I've got to acknowledge I see proverbial sparks flying whenever you two are around each other.''

"Don't be silly. The truth is Grady's anxious for me to leave. I'd hate to think my presence drove Libby away from here.''

Noel shrugged. "The way Shady Pointe is, she's probably better off.''

"And I have to visit her class this afternoon. How am I going to face her?''

Noel leaned forward, propping his elbows on his

long legs. ''Kate, I don't know Libby very well. But I guess I should tell you the rest of it.''

Kate arched her brow. ''Well?''

''It's probably only a rumor. But Chelsea says another teacher who is supposed to be Libby's close friend claims Libby's using the job offer as an ultimatum to Grady. Either he proposes or she leaves.''

Kate's eyes widened. Libby didn't seem the kind of woman who would use such strong-arm tactics, but then Kate didn't know her well. Was that why Grady had been pressuring her about her feelings? Was he trying to make sure once and for all before he asked Libby to marry him that he was doing the right thing?

''Grady wouldn't let himself be manipulated that way,'' she concluded.

''I know you better than I know Libby, and I can't believe you're just going to sit back without a fight.''

''If he loves her, Noel, there's nothing I can do about it.''

''I suppose you're right. I only hope he realizes he doesn't love her. Grady's always been big on home and family. I'd hate to see him settle for the wrong thing.''

''How can you be so sure he doesn't love her?''

''Because he's like you. Stubborn enough to be loyal to the one person he really loves no matter what. Why don't you two stop all this dancing around and find a little happiness?''

Kate shook her head. ''Grady knows what he wants,

Noel," she reflected. "Whether Libby goes or stays won't make any difference between us. There's no possibility of our having a future together. And I refuse to believe Libby would pressure Grady that way. She seems too nice."

Later, as she drove toward the elementary school, her stomach was in knots. Whatever mixed feelings she harbored toward Libby, she couldn't let them show.

Walking down the wide corridor in the school brought back a flood of old memories. The building smelled of paste and crayons and school lunches. Wreaths made of red and green construction paper adorned the bulletin boards.

As advised by a sign at the entrance, she stopped at the office to check in. The school secretary contacted Libby on the intercom.

She smiled up at Kate. "Go on down. It's the third door on the right."

Libby, standing at the front of her classroom, spotted Kate approaching and welcomed her with a smile and a wave. *She* is *nice,* Kate reaffirmed. Only a selfish shrew could resent this pleasant young woman, she admonished herself. She took a deep breath before entering the room.

Thirty small, rapt faces were staring up at her expectantly.

Libby introduced her as the creator of Calico Chrissie and told the students they could ask questions one at a time if they raised their hands. She offered Kate a chair at the front of the room. She set the tote bag she'd brought in on top of Libby's desk.

Kate was amazed at the range of questions they asked. Most centered around dolls; a few were about life in New York. She tried to answer as honestly and simply as she could.

"How did you start making dolls?" a cherubic-faced girl asked.

Kate smiled. She reached for her tote bag and began taking out fabric pieces she'd packed earlier. The students leaned forward in their seats.

"When I was a little girl growing up here in Shady Pointe, just like all of you, I played with dolls and pretended they were real little people. As I got older, I learned to sew, and I discovered I could take scraps of material and thread and make dolls that looked just the way I wanted them to."

She held up the head and body she'd assembled earlier, taking needle and thread and demonstrating how she could stitch them together to make a rag doll.

As she stitched, she continued fielding their questions. Even the boys seemed interested. But she balked when one round-faced little boy raised his hand and innocently asked, "What's it like to be in a plane crash?" Her tongue suddenly thickened and she nearly stuck her finger with the needle.

Of course, they knew from watching television and

listening to their parents. As she hesitated, she saw Libby's expression narrow with concern.

She realized as long as she shied away from talking about it, people were always going to be wondering, treating her with solicitous caution.

"Very frightening," she admitted. "But fortunately, such accidents are extremely rare." Skipping the details of her experience, she launched into statistics on the safety of air travel.

As she wound up her talk, mothers began arriving with paper cups and jugs of punch and home-baked iced cookies. Seeing she was losing her audience's attention, she quickly concluded.

Libby rushed up to her, setting a hand on her arm. "That was wonderful, Kate," she complimented her as the mothers served the refreshments. "You will stay for our party, won't you? It's the last day of school."

Kate stayed. She drank punch and ate cookies and felt a little like she'd gone back to third grade. She chatted with the mothers, making a point of announcing how happy she was to be back in Shady Pointe and that she was looking forward to attending the community caroling.

After the bell rang and the room cleared, Kate found Libby staring at her.

"You're staying here, aren't you?" Libby asked.

Kate blinked innocently. "What makes you say that?"

"You're going to a lot of trouble to undermine the boycott."

"The caroling is a local tradition. I don't think it's the proper forum for a political statement."

"Does Grady know?"

"That I'm recruiting people to attend the caroling? I didn't know myself I was doing it until a few minutes ago. If people can put their differences aside for a couple of hours, it'll be a start in turning this town in the right direction."

"Yes, I suppose it might. But I meant, does Grady know you're staying here?"

"I don't think I knew that either until you said it. But my decision isn't connected to Grady. He's been a big help to me these past few days, allowing me to use his cabin. Actually, I guess I'm staying despite Grady."

"That's funny. He adores you, you know."

Kate felt her face redden.

"No. You're mistaken. I have no intention of coming between the two of you."

Libby looked bewildered. Then she laughed. "Kate, you're the one who's mistaken. Grady and I have gone out together off and on for the past couple of years, and we've become good friends. I don't know how I would have survived here if he hadn't taken me under his wing."

"Taken you under his wing?"

"He and my older brother were roommates in vet

school. When I took a job here, my brother told me to be sure and look Grady up. I sure appreciated Grady. Here I was, away from my family for the first time, so he took me over to his parents' house a lot. I guess they all kind of adopted me. But there's never been any serious attachment between the two of us. We're good friends, so it's been convenient to go places together. In fact, when I went home on vacation last summer, I met someone I'm interested in, which is one of the reasons I've taken a job back there. I never got over being homesick. Grady's probably tired of listening to me talk about how much I miss being home. I just don't see a future for myself in Shady Pointe.''

Kate lowered her gaze. Could Grady have been talking about Libby the other day, not her? ''Why are you explaining all this?''

''Because Grady can't take his eyes off you when you walk into a room. I've never seen him look at anybody that way. I was afraid I was standing between the two of you. I'm surprised he didn't explain he and I are simply friends.''

Kate shook her head. ''I never gave him a chance. I appreciate your honesty, Libby. But I'm afraid the problems between Grady and me run deeper than that. Maybe we're too much alike, independent and strong-willed.''

Libby shrugged and began picking up paper plates off the desks. ''Two people as smart as you and

Grady, I wouldn't think any obstacle could have the two of you stumped.''

In her car alone, as she headed toward town, Kate realized she'd suspected all along that Grady and Libby had no commitment to each other. If they had, Grady would never have kissed her. When he gave his word, he kept it. Perhaps she'd been too overwhelmed by her own feelings to acknowledge that.

A wet snow began to fall, and she flipped on the windshield wipers. She didn't have Libby to use as an excuse to shield herself from Grady anymore. If only she dared face him with the acceptance she'd opened herself to by the creek yesterday. But she wasn't free to tell Grady how she felt. Maybe she had too much pride for her own good.

Chapter Ten

" "I'll see you at the community caroling tomorrow night then," Kate reminded Mrs. Ziffretti as the elderly store owner wrapped the platter Kate had selected for her mother.

The older woman shot her a blank look. "Haven't you heard? No one's going except Hewett Sparks and his supporters. Perhaps he'll catch on folks around here aren't too pleased that this town's falling to pieces. Maybe he'll see how few residents actually back him."

Kate smiled brightly, accepting the proffered package and stuffing it in her shopping bag with her other purchases. "Seems like all the more reason people around here should want to pull together. That's why

I decided to do all my Christmas shopping right here in town. If there's one thing I've missed about Shady Pointe, it was everyone getting together right before Christmas and singing with their neighbors. It didn't matter where you lived or worked or how much money or influence you had. As a child I believed, at least for a while, that we all liked one another. That's what made Shady Pointe special. Oh, well, I guess it's time to stop deluding myself. This town has changed while I was away. But I'll be there singing my fool head off anyway. I always get the shivers when Mrs. Osgood plays 'What Child Is This' on the piano.''

''Oh, my!''

''What's wrong? Don't they sing that anymore?''

''Mabel isn't going to play this year. She wasn't planning on coming to the caroling at all.''

Kate frowned. ''Why not? She's not ill, is she?''

''No. It's just . . . some trouble between her and the Sparkses. Well, never mind. I'll talk to her.''

''I really hope I'll see you there. I've just about made up my mind not to go back to New York.''

''You're staying, Kate?'' What will you do?''

Kate shrugged. ''There's a lot that needs doing here. I'm sure I'll find something.''

In the long run, her company would go on under new management. Life in New York would go on as always without her. Here, she had a chance to make a difference. Shady Pointe needed her, and that was important.

A grin crossed the older woman's face. "Does anyone know? You can't imagine what a boost your staying on will give us, Kate. Maybe you could run for mayor."

"No, I'm afraid I'll be too busy. I'll have to find a place to live and a way to make a living. Someone who's better established in the community would make a better candidate."

"If you need help with anything, you just call me, honey."

Kate smiled. Mrs. Ziffretti's eagerness brought to mind memories of the Shady Pointe she'd grown up in.

"Merry Christmas, Mrs. Ziffretti!" Kate called as she left the shop.

Mrs. Ziffretti was lifting the telephone receiver before the front door closed.

Kate beamed with satisfaction. If anyone stayed away from this year's caroling, their absence would scarcely be noticed. Grady would not be pleased, but he'd just have to find another way to express his views.

Out on the street, she found herself searching for signs of the reporter. She was getting weary of hiding from him. Relieved, she saw no one watching her. Maybe he'd given up and gone home for the holidays. Surely he must have a family somewhere.

Stashing her purchases in the back of Grady's Explorer, she started back to the lake. She'd meant to stop back by her parents' house and see if they were home now, but she decided instead to fix a light dinner and spend the evening wrapping her gifts.

After the holiday, she'd have to return briefly to New York to wrap up her business there and sublet her apartment. And she had much to sort out. Where would she live in Shady Pointe? She couldn't impose on her parents indefinitely. And what kind of business could she start here that would help the town grow?

When she reached the cabin, the light was fading. Wet snow, more like sleet, continued falling intermittently. She was surprised to spot her car parked out front.

Grady. Her heart soared. He'd come to see her after all, at last.

As she got out, he emerged from the woods, looking grim.

Her smile dropped.

''What's wrong, Grady?'' she asked, rushing toward him.

''Where's Ollie?'' he demanded.

''He's in the cabin. I'm sure he's frantic to be let out . . .''

''He's not inside. When you weren't here, I unlocked the door to let him out while I was waiting for you. He's not here.''

Kate paled. ''He was in there when I left.''

''He couldn't have gotten out on his own. You must have left him outside. How long were you away?''

"Hours," she confessed in a shrinking voice. She searched her memory. Had she accidentally left Ollie outside? She thought of the thin ice crusting the lake.

Grady's intent, accusing glare curdled her blood.

"I'll help you look for him," she offered. "It'll be dark soon."

Without waiting for an answer, she raced toward the lake. She found no sign of Ollie, but at least she didn't see any large patches of broken ice. Who knew how far he could have walked out before it gave way? A shiver raced up her spine. Big, stupid dog. Nuisance that he was, he had kept her laughing these past few days. He *had* to be all right.

"Ollie!" she called. In the distance, she heard Grady whistling for his dog.

Calling until her throat was raw, she scoured the bushes until darkness made it impossible to see. Grady came up behind her, halting her frantic movements with a hand on her arm.

"Give it up, Katie. He's either long gone or can't hear us." Defeat deepened his voice.

She turned to him. "I know he was in there when I left, Grady."

"Couldn't you have let him out and forgotten about him? I should have stopped to think you're not used to watching out for an animal. I never should have left him out here. I was thinking about your welfare, and I forgot you didn't like him."

Katie craned her neck incredulously. Here she was

feeling miserable because she'd grown attached to Ollie and his antics, and Grady was accusing her of intentionally losing him.

"That's not fair! Even if I thought he was the most
vile creature on earth, I wouldn't have left him running
loose. If I was tired of his company, I would have
called you to come and get him. If that's how far apart
we are, that you think me capable of losing your dog
on purpose, I don't want to stay in your cabin anymore. I'm leaving tonight, and you can drive your Explorer back to town too."

"Now wait, Katie. I'm not going to throw you out
because of this."

"Well, if I run into that reporter I'll give him a
piece of my mind too. I can handle the wolves on my
own, thank you. I wonder how many people would
want to vote for you if they knew the real Grady Meredith. Great guy. When it comes to anything that really
counts, you don't give an inch, do you? You know I
wouldn't have left your dog out, and just because
I can't explain what happened to him, you assume I
must be responsible. Good night, Grady. Here, take
your keys. I'll lock up when I leave."

She packed hurriedly, anxious to be free of the
cabin. When she saw Grady still sitting out front in
his Explorer, she wondered if he'd stayed behind to
check that she had locked the door. But he started his
engine when she got in her car. Had he stayed to en-

sure she left safely, or was he hoping for a sign of Ollie?

Watching him sitting alone in the darkness, she felt a pang of sympathy. She knew how protective Grady had always felt toward animals. But he should have seen she too was worried about Ollie, instead of blaming her.

Driving back to her parents' house, she felt desolate and empty inside. Poor Ollie. How had he gotten out? Where was he?

Her parents were delighted by her return. After unpacking, she had dinner with them, then insisted her mother relax while she cleaned the kitchen. Later, she declined their invitation to watch a television movie with them and went upstairs to wrap gifts. The activity failed to lift her spirits.

The phone rang downstairs, and her mom called up to her. Wondering who was calling, she went to the kitchen and lifted the receiver.

''Hello?''

''Someone here wants to speak to you,'' Grady announced.

Waiting for a voice to come on the line, she heard only a faint jingling sound. Dog tags.

''What in—Ollie!''

Grady came back on the line. ''I found him in the yard a few minutes ago.''

''Oh, Grady, I'm so glad he's all right—'' Remembering their harsh exchange earlier, she broke off her words.

"Katie, I'm sorry I blamed you. I was upset that he was missing, and I shouldn't have taken it out on you."

"No, it had to be my fault. He must have slipped out the door behind me or something."

"Katie, I do know you wouldn't be careless enough to have let him out intentionally. You're right. I shouldn't have doubted that."

"Forget it. I'm just glad he's home."

"Actually, it was more than just being worried about the dog. I feel like you've put this wall up between us."

"I know."

A long silence spun over the telephone line.

"You can go back to the cabin if you want," Grady offered finally.

"No. I'm not running away anymore. I meant what I said about that reporter. It was time for me to leave the cabin anyway."

She thought she heard him chuckle. "Good night, Katie," he said.

Distractedly, she replaced the receiver. Geographically, he was only a few miles away. But as far as she was concerned, it might as well have been a million. And she knew their truce was only temporary. Grady was not going to be pleased when he discovered she was unraveling his protest against Hewett Sparks. Her decision to stay in Shady Pointe would probably only push her and Grady farther apart.

When Kate stepped through the double doors leading into the auditorium of the Congregational Church, her heart leapt into her throat. As she'd anticipated from the smattering of cars parked in the lot, the crowd was pitifully small. Hewett and Evie Sparks stood in one corner of the room, a few of their friends gathered around them.

Disappointment dampened her spirits. She'd spent the entire day driving around town, chatting with her neighbors and dropping pointed hints that she hoped to see them at this evening's caroling. Apparently, no one could muster enough holiday goodwill to put politics aside for one night. Things in Shady Pointe had gotten worse than she'd suspected.

And to complicate matters, toward late afternoon, she'd spotted a dark van behind her car.

Now, Hewett Sparks waved to her. Halfheartedly, she waved back. Maybe her staying here wouldn't make a difference after all. She'd been foolish to expect to start changing things overnight.

The festive decorations—red and white poinsettias and evergreen garlands woven with red ribbons and tiny white lights—failed to lighten her mood. What was wrong with these people? It was Christmas, after all. Life was too short to harbor such pettiness toward one another.

Too short to live without Grady because her pride demanded more than he could give her?

Heading for the coat room, she pushed that disturbing thought out of her mind. She had to concentrate on doing what was best for the town, not on her feelings for Grady.

Carefully, she took off her wool coat and hung it up, revealing a red satin dress trimmed with white lace. Her hair, pulled into a twist, was flecked with silver glitter. She had worked hard to put herself in a holiday mood. Still, she didn't feel very sparkling on the inside.

"You look terrific," a voice came from behind her.

Kate turned. "Noel!" she exclaimed.

"You seem surprised to see me."

"It's just that I've been hearing rumblings about a protest tonight."

"I heard that too. But I'm just visiting here. It's got nothing to do with me. Besides, I heard you've been running around town urging everyone to show up. Since we're friends and all, I thought . . ."

She gave him a quick hug. "You remember how this town used to be, don't you? All this dissension makes me sad."

He nodded. "Times change. I'd like to see it preserved the way it used to be, but there's no way it will ever be the same. What's this I heard about you're telling people you're staying here?"

She shrugged. "Pretty wild, isn't it?"

"I can't imagine coming back here to stay."

Kate's eyes widened. "I know. I felt the same way once upon a time. You look pretty sharp tonight yourself." He'd traded his usual jeans for dress slacks and had gone so far as to wear a tie. He looked lean and handsome and more mature.

"Thanks," he said, bowing his head self-consciously. "We'd better get back out to the party. Everyone's going to be expecting you."

"Didn't you notice there's no one here?"

Noel stuck his hands in his pockets and shook his head. "Because you're twenty minutes early and this is Shady Pointe. Have you forgotten how fashionable it is to be late here?"

She laughed lightly. "Do you really think they'll come?"

"I know Mabel Osgood changed her mind about playing the piano tonight. That's an encouraging sign. Now, come on. Whether you know it or not, this is your party."

Only a few more people had come in. Kate mingled with the people she recognized, her spirits lifting as she greeted Mrs. Ziffretti and Chandler McCorey, people she knew were opposed to Hewett Sparks. When Mabel Osgood came through the door, Kate rushed up to meet her.

Noel had been right—people began streaming in. Kate waved to a mother she'd met in Libby's class-room. She was amazed to recall how awkward she'd felt in a crowd just a few weeks ago. Now, a serenity and a sense of belonging came over her. She knew she was where she was meant to be.

Glancing up, she did a double take as she spied what appeared to be a younger version of Grady coming through the door. The face was the same, but the walk was less forceful. He came toward her.

"Hi, Katie. I guess you remember me."

"Sure, Kenny. Hello. It's good to see you."

She looked up at the strapping young man, finding it hard to believe he'd survived a brain tumor, that his parents had feared he'd never live past his teens. Yet standing before her was living proof that miracles do happen.

"I'm glad I ran into you. I wanted to apologize."

Kate's brow furrowed. She hadn't seen Kenny in years; what could he possibly need to apologize for? "To me?" she asked.

"I didn't know until I saw Grady in town today that you were staying in his cabin at the lake. I went out there yesterday to get Mom some wood for the fireplace, and the minute I opened the door, Ollie zipped past me and he wouldn't come back. I couldn't figure out what he was doing out there all by himself anyway. When I started back he was walking down the road, and when I stopped and opened the door of my truck, he jumped right in. I dropped him off inside the fence at Grady's house on my way back into town.

Grady seemed really upset when I told him about it this afternoon.''

"He was frantic when we couldn't find Ollie. Don't worry about it, Kenny. But I do appreciate your clearing up the mystery.''

People began drifting into seats so the program could begin. Kate accepted a photocopied song sheet, although she knew the words to all the carols by heart. Noel and Chelsea had saved her a seat near the front.

Kate heard a sudden rumbling ripple through the crowd and felt Noel nudge her shoulder. Looking up to see faces turned back toward the doorway, she followed their glances to the entrance. James Foley, slicked up in a black suit he probably wore mostly to funerals, stood in front of the door, scowling as he scanned the room.

Mr. Foley had lived next door to Kate's parents as long as she could remember, and she'd never seen him at the caroling or any local activity.

When his small eyes lit on her and he headed in her direction, her stomach knotted. His expression was so fierce, she wondered if she'd accidentally piled snow on his lawn.

To her utter astonishment, the little man took the empty folding chair beside her, mustering a grotesque facsimile of a smile. ''Heard you might stay,'' he said.

Kate suppressed a sudden urge to cry. That this man she'd always believed hated everybody had thought enough of her to put his suit on and show up tonight to encourage her to stay meant more to her than she could say.

A hush fell over the room, and she looked up through misty eyes to see Mabel Osgood at the piano. The first chords rang out.

As the songs began, Kate struggled with the hot tears stinging her eyes. She was lucky to be among people who had overcome their differences to be here tonight simply because she'd asked them to. Times might be tough in Shady Pointe, but she couldn't help feeling optimistic. If people cared enough to work together . . .

A familiar, slightly off-key baritone boomed from the back of the room, joining the other voices.

Katie snapped her head around. Her eyes met Grady's, and she felt a tug in her heart. He had come, after all. Grady always did try to do the right thing.

Smiling softly, she showed her gratitude in her eyes.

Grady was smiling back as he sang. She saw the pride in his face, and her pulse quickened as she realized it was directed at her.

Love swelled inside her. If only . . . No, she couldn't think about that now.

She turned back around to face the front. Grady would never abandon his principles. But he had opened his mind enough to see dividing the town wouldn't help anyone. Maybe Hewett Sparks wasn't an effective mayor anymore. But his experience could still be a valuable contribution. He could help whoever took over leadership in the spring. Kate realized her absence had given her enough objectivity to deal with the problems here effectively. She felt the heat of Grady's eyes on her back. Her soul seemed to rise with the crest of the music and the joyous blend of voices.

The town was facing its problems. Could she and Grady face theirs?

She would start her new life here by coming clean with him. Later, she would admit her feelings openly and honestly. She would tell him why she'd really had to leave so many years ago and why they couldn't be together now.

The singing seemed to last forever. As much as she enjoyed it, Kate grew fidgety, anxious.

Then, as the crowd dispersed and people drifted toward the refreshment table, she scanned the crowd for Grady. He seemed to have been swallowed up in the mass of people.

''Katie!'' She turned as she heard him calling her name. He placed a cup of eggnog in her hand.

''Thanks,'' she said. It was impossible to be heard over the din of voices. Someone pushed passed her, nearly knocking the cup out of her hand.

Grady looked at her, about to speak, when the sound of his name being called rang above the buzz of the crowd.

Mr. Foley was standing beside him, trying to get his attention. ''I'm sorry about your dog,'' he said, speaking loud enough to be heard over the crowd. "I wouldn't have killed him. It was just a BB gun."

Grady nodded and patted the old man's shoulder.

After he'd disappeared back into the crowd, Grady turned to her again. He said something indiscernible.

Kate raised her palm in the air to indicate she had no idea what he'd said.

He leaned down over her shoulder. The heat of his skin radiated against her cheek, and she smelled a mixture of soap and spicy after-shave.

"Let's go somewhere and talk," he said into her ear. "Please."

As she was nodding her agreement, the sight of a medium-built man standing to one side of the long table paralyzed her. His piercing eyes and dark goatee were hauntingly familiar. They should be. He'd been following her for some time now.

Grady followed her gaze, and fury darkened his expression.

But as quickly as Grady started toward the man, she caught his arm, halting him.

Grady looked on, bewildered, as Katie approached the man, who was looking at the floor, trying to pretend he didn't see her.

"Excuse me," she said.

When he failed to look up, she repeated herself.

He raised his eyes guiltily.

She extended her hand. "I'm Kate Smithers," she told him.

"Mike Duncan," he replied hesitantly, accepting her handshake.

"What publication do you write for, Mike?"

He hesitated, then told her.

"Well," she said, "I'm not giving any interviews, but I hope you'll write about what a nice place my hometown is. You should meet everyone here, since you're crashing their gathering. Shouldn't you be at home with your family? Tomorrow's Christmas Eve. Would you like some eggnog and cookies?"

When she looked up, she realized the room had fallen silent, and every eye in the room was turned toward her as she led the sheepish-looking reporter to the refreshment table.

Mrs. Sparks sprang forward. "Here, son, let me get you a plate. You have to try some of Mrs. Henderson's seven-layer dip."

The other townspeople, taking her cue, converged around him, fussing and loading his plate up with portions of everything on the table. Mrs. Ziffretti was ladling eggnog.

Kate backed off, jumping at a tap on her shoulder. Grady stood behind her. He had his coat on and was holding hers.

Flashing a conspiratorial smile, she allowed him to help her slide into it. He took hold of her hand as they slipped out the side door into the frozen night. Fat snowflakes were fluttering through the air.

Without slowing down, Grady turned the corner into

the parking lot. He stopped, leaning his back against the brick wall. Kate was laughing and trying to catch her breath at the same time. Suddenly, the night bristled with magic. Wonder and anticipation filled Kate's heart, and she realized only now did it truly feel like Christmas. And she was daring to be happy without browbeating herself with guilt.

Slowly, Grady turned to face her. The snow was falling so hard, it matted on Kate's eyelashes.

Blinking back snowflakes, she waited for him to speak. "They'll be feeding him for hours," he said, finally.

"I just hope Mr. Foley doesn't go home and get his BB gun."

Grady's deep laugh echoed through the night air. "You handled that beautifully. Seeing you tonight, well, you seem more the way I remember you."

"But I'm not the same," she assured him quickly. "Do you remember when I fell out of the apple tree in your yard?"

"Do I! I was sure you must have broken your neck."

"I remember hitting the ground hard and then looking up and seeing you kneeling over me with that worried look on your face. I was too young to put a name to the way I felt about you back then, but when I saw you, I knew I was okay, that the bad part was over."

"But when I tried to help you up, you pushed me away. Why?"

"Damaged pride. I was embarrassed for falling. Grady, when I came back here to sort things out, I gave myself a lot of reasons for doing so. One of them I wouldn't admit to was I needed to see you again. I *have* missed you."

A shadow crossed his expression, then he looked at her as if he were about to speak. To her surprised delight, he kept his words to himself and instead folded her into his arms and gave her a kiss as velvet as the night.

"I wish you'd come with us to the Dunmores'," Julia Smithers insisted as she and her husband were leaving. "You shouldn't spend Christmas Eve alone."

"I'll be fine, Mom," Kate assured her. "I have some things I need to do. Don't worry. I'm not staying here to sulk."

"I know. It's really good to have you acting more like yourself again. For a while there, you were so quiet and subdued . . . Well, we won't be too late."

"You don't have to hurry back on my account. Enjoy yourselves. Just be careful driving."

When they were gone, Kate poured herself a glass of diet cola and went to the kitchen. She began pulling out the ingredients for the jelled salad she'd promised to make for tomorrow's dinner.

But her mind was on Grady, not salad. How wonderful it had felt last night to rest in his strong arms as they sheltered her from the snow. Desperately, she had tried to tell him what was in her heart, but he hadn't given her the chance.

The Merediths' house across the street was lit up brighter than the Christmas tree in the living room. She knew he was probably there, with his family.

When the doorbell rang, she shot out of her chair.

Grady and Ollie stood side by side.

"Merry Christmas," Grady greeted her. He pressed a wrapped package into her hands.

"Come on in," she invited, stepping aside.

After instructing Ollie to stay, he came in the house.

"I'm glad you came by. I have something for you too."

"Katie, about last night . . ."

She shook her head as she searched the pile of gifts under the tree for his.

"I guess we were both taken in by all the emotion. Friends and enemies coming together. It was pretty moving, wasn't it?"

"You made it happen, Katie."

Spotting his gift, she grabbed it. Walking back to him, she placed it in his hands.

"No, I only put the idea in their heads. The people who made the effort to come, they made it happen. I can't tell you, Grady, what your being there meant to me."

"People are expecting big things from you. Rumor has it you're staying."

"I am. That's not going to bother you, is it?"

"Hewett Sparks says Mike whatever-his-name-was checked out of the motel this morning. At least he won't be bothering you."

"Grady, I asked you if my staying here was going to disturb you."

"Of course it is."

Kate was taken aback. "Well, then you're not going to like what I'm going to say."

"Oh, here it comes. Katie the steamroller. You've always thought you could do everything on your own. What was I supposed to do? You said, 'I love you, Grady, but I've got to go to New York.' What's it going to be now—'I love you Grady, but I've got to put the town back together?' And I know you still love me, even if you won't say it. Do you know how many times I've mentally kicked myself for not telling you how much I needed you here? I'd never lost anyone close to me, and I thought my little brother was going to die. I couldn't have been so unfair as to drag you into all that. I always thought there'd be time later, that you'd be back at least to visit and I'd have more to offer you."

She looked into his rich, compelling eyes. "I thought you let me go because you didn't need me."

"Not need the only person in the world willing to go door-to-door with me finding homes for stray puppies?" he asked.

"Aren't you going to open your gift?"

He tore the paper off the box, extracting a limp, gaudy fishing hat.

"It's almost like my old one. I'd forgotten about that thing." His eyes narrowed. "But you didn't."

"I love you, Grady," she told him, her heart galloping. "Listen, what I said earlier about us not being right for each other, I'm not so sure . . ."

"It took me a while to catch on to your thinking something serious was going on between me and Libby. Actually, I had been trying to persuade her to stay, because she's a good teacher. But after she accepted her new job, I realized she'd be happier back home."

"Which you were telling my mom on Sunday. Grady, I thought you were saying you wanted *me* to leave."

He grinned. "I see that didn't deter you from staying. I think you'd better open your gift. I can't stand the suspense much longer."

She flashed him a quizzical look. Judging by the box's size and shape, she was pretty sure it contained the brooch she'd admired in Mrs. Ziffretti's shop. She wasn't well practiced at feigning surprise.

As she'd anticipated, the box held the brooch.

"I did like this a lot," she said.

"You have to lift it out of the box to really appreciate it," he told her.

Perplexed, she did as he instructed, revealing the delicate circle of gold and diamonds beneath it.

She turned wide, startled eyes to him.

"I don't suppose life with a country vet could sound too intriguing to someone who's dined with movie stars," he hedged.

Her eyes darkened. "Try me."

"Marry me, Katie. And if you want to work in New York or Alaska, we'll work it out somehow. I mean, I have to stay here until my clinic's paid off, but later I can sell it. We can live wherever you want."

"Echo Lake?" she asked.

"I'd like very much to live at Echo Lake."

"Then I'd be honored to marry you."

He leaned forward slowly, sealing their pledge with a poignant kiss.

"There's just one problem," he added, as she settled happily into his embrace.

"What more could there be?" she asked, alarmed.

"Who are we going to get to run for mayor?"

"I was thinking of Mrs. Ziffretti."

"You might be onto something."

Kate looked past his shoulder into the orange firelight and the shimmering tree in the darkened living room, and she realized those small brilliant lights shone brightest in the dark of winter if only you looked hard enough to see them. She had a life full of loving to look forward to, and she was grateful not only for a second chance but having found the strength to take it.

CHARLOTTE COUNTY LIBRARY
CHARLOTTE COURT HOUSE, VIRGINIA

DEMCO